The baby was gurgling behind Justin, but other than that there was only the sound of his breathing.

He was close enough that she felt the movements of his chest with every breath. Warmth licked through her as their eyes met, and the heat in his gaze incinerated the grin right off her face. His hair was soft under her fingers, his body hot as it pressed into hers, his mouth sweet and urgent, and somehow the universe was finally just as it should be.

The baby interrupted, her soft gurgles changing into a whine that told them she would be wanting some attention very soon.

The kiss ended, but their embrace didn't. Not right away.

"Laura..." he whispered, his mouth at her ear, and his arms tightened around her. She turned her face into his neck, and felt at home. In fact she felt...in love.

Things were getting *way* out of hand.

Hannah Bernard always knew what she wanted to be when she grew up—a psychologist. After spending an eternity in university studying toward that goal, she took one look at her hard-earned diploma and thought, "Nah. I'd rather be a writer."

She has no kids to brag about, no pets to complain about and only one husband, who any day now will break down and agree to adopt a kitten.

Their Accidental Baby is Hannah's second book for Harlequin Romance.

Books by Hannah Bernard

THEIR
ACCIDENTAL BABY
Hannah Bernard

TANGO
IT TAKES TWO...

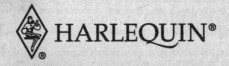

HARLEQUIN®

TORONTO • NEW YORK • LONDON
AMSTERDAM • PARIS • SYDNEY • HAMBURG
STOCKHOLM • ATHENS • TOKYO • MILAN • MADRID
PRAGUE • WARSAW • BUDAPEST • AUCKLAND

To everyone at eHarlequin.com's WR board.
May SubCare always bounce with happy news.

ISBN 0-373-03774-0

THEIR ACCIDENTAL BABY

First North American Publication 2003.

Copyright © 2003 by Hannah Bernard.

This edition published by arrangement with Harlequin Books S.A.

® and TM are trademarks of the publisher. Trademarks indicated with ® are registered in the United States Patent and Trademark Office, the Canadian Trade Marks Office and in other countries.

Visit us at www.eHarlequin.com

Printed in U.S.A.

CHAPTER ONE

LAURA tilted her head back and peered upward at the path ahead, shoulders slumped in fatigue. Endlessly stretching toward the summit, the way up looked exhausting and treacherous.

But at journey's end, there was sanctuary.

This wasn't exactly Mount Everest. Just an apartment building in Chicago's suburbs. All she had to do was climb three floors, and she would get to her cozy little apartment, close the door and forget all about there being a world outside.

The shades of the maples lining the quiet street gave testament to it already being autumn. And here she'd hardly noticed the summer, except as a hot distraction; a need to daily give thanks for the air-conditioning in her office; and the lingering smell of barbecue in the air as she dragged herself home late at night.

There just weren't enough Fridays in a week.

Weekend.

For once she wasn't working at all. She didn't even have any homework to do. Two days off, to do anything she wanted. She could take a long bubble bath, put soft music on the stereo and daydream. She could pick a book from the huge pile that somehow had taken up permanent residence in her laundry basket and read—if she could keep her eyes open. She could shake the dust off that sweater she'd started to knit before Young & Warren had hired her six months ago. Or she could call

5

some of those friends who probably assumed she was dead and buried and they'd missed the funeral.

Of course, there was also housework. She'd run out of dishes for her morning cereal three days ago. Not that it had mattered much, since the milk had gone bad a few days before.

She hadn't even had clean underwear this morning and, after twenty seconds of torturous deliberations, had decided to go without.

Bad idea.

After a whole morning of sitting in meetings, imagining that everyone present had to know this scandalous fact, could see it on her face, if not on her bottom, she'd used her ten-minute lunch break to run to the nearest store and buy a multipack of cheap underwear that would see her through the next week. Putting them on in the tiny cubicle that served as the ladies' room had been a feat that would have earned her the praise of her yoga instructor—if she still had the time to attend classes.

But at least now she knew. The women's magazines lied. Going without underwear did not make you feel sexy. Just uncomfortable and naked.

If she could have spared more than ten minutes, she wouldn't currently be wearing green and pink cotton underpants with smiley faces and writing on them. In French. She'd never learned any French, but considering the cheap price and the location in the discount bin, she could only hazard a guess that it said something women generally did not want written on their underwear.

Not that it mattered. It wasn't as if anyone was seeing her underwear these days, let alone anyone who spoke French. She grimaced. Life was so busy right now that it was as well that Mr. Right wasn't showing up. She'd just have to shoo him away and ask him to come back later.

"Hi. Bye." Justin Bane, her neighbor, rushed past her, a blurry figure in black leaving behind the warm scent of leather and sandalwood, and had vanished farther up the stairs before she'd even drawn breath to return his greeting.

Of course he could move fast. He wasn't wearing heels. Or green underwear with coded messages in French. He didn't work her hours, either. He even had the energy to sing in the shower, and he was used to moving fast on that motorbike. Nope, three flights of stairs wouldn't be a problem for him.

Ten steps up, seventy to go. She took another deep breath and pulled herself up one more step with a mighty groan. She'd moved to the suburbs to get away from a tiny apartment overlooking two major streets, but what had possessed her to rent an apartment on the third floor, in a building where the elevator was always on the fritz? Right, she'd been young and stupid six months ago. Convinced she could handle anything the world threw at her, even a daily trek up three flights of stairs, now that she had finally landed her dream job.

She sighed. Dreams weren't all they were cracked up to be. Eighty-hour weeks and extinct weekends hadn't figured prominently in her fantasies during those long years in law school.

Housework probably couldn't be avoided. But not tonight. And not tomorrow. Maybe Sunday she'd feel up to challenging tasks like loading the washing machine or the dishwasher. Tonight she'd order takeout and camp out in front of the television until reality blurred into a

Hollywood fantasy and she forgot all about legal briefs, courtrooms, divorces and custody battles.

Her stomach growled.

Food. Oh, yes, that was another plan for this weekend. There had hardly been time to eat at all this week. Or last weekend, or the week before. Fruit or candy bars stuffed in her mouth while running between weekends had been a luxury. Hot meals were just a distant memory. Her mouth watered just at the thought of cooking aromas and the imagined calories gave her enough energy to conquer a few more steps.

Of course, she passed Justin's apartment on the way to her door every evening, and her nose told her he did not make do with fruit and candy bars. He seemed fond of spicy chicken and home cooked pizza, the smells making her stomach whine in yearning and her own pinnacle of kitchen achievements—grilled cheese sandwiches—taste like recycled paper.

Her stomach growled again, and she winced at the hunger pangs, promising to eat properly this weekend. Perhaps she should invite a friend over, and cook something ambitious. Hamburgers, perhaps. Or grilled cheese sandwiches with actual cheese in them.

Of course that meant she had to go shopping too.

She groaned, and used the impetus of the unwelcome thought to propel her up another step, which took her up to the first floor. She was one third of the way up. She celebrated by leaning against the wall and closing her eyes for a bit. Tomorrow she'd think about shopping. Tonight she wouldn't do anything at all. Getting home was challenge enough.

Two floors to go.

"Are you sick?"

The voice was only inches away. She forced her eyes open, and looked into concerned dark eyes. She shook her head slowly in response to his inquiry. Justin, again. She hadn't even heard him run down the stairs. And there was no question that he had run. He always moved fast.

The leather jacket gone, he stood there in a crumpled black shirt and black jeans, hands in his pockets as he loomed over her, even though she was wearing those dreadful heels. She tried not to inhale. That one sniff of male pheromones as he'd rushed past her on his way up had been enough of a mocking temptation for one day, and she hadn't even seen him dismount his bike this time.

She'd never had much of a thing for motorbikes, but boy, did this one wear them well.

She stared up into those dark brown eyes and inwardly stomped on that reluctant crush she'd had on him ever since he'd moved in. It was absurd. She was much too old to have crushes.

Wasn't she?

Justin touched her forehead for a second as if to check for fever, then lifted her head to look into her eyes. He grabbed her wrist and put his fingers on her pulse. What was he, a doctor? Someone had told her he was a teacher, but he didn't look much like any teacher she'd ever had. Perhaps they'd been wrong, and he was really a doctor. Maybe if she stopped breathing, he'd resort to the kiss of life. Not an altogether unpleasant notion.

Justin frowned. ''Laura, your pulse is racing. And unless you're running up and down the stairs for exercise, you've been more than five minutes just getting up to here. What's wrong?''

Justin the gallant neighbor, coming to the rescue, completely unaware that her pulse had a crush on him, and had started galloping at his touch. What next? She had visions of him sweeping her up in his arms and carrying her up to her apartment, where he'd carefully lay her down on the couch.

She closed her eyes to better concentrate on the fantasy. His arms would be strong but gentle, his movements sure and confident, an intimate look in those dark eyes and a sensual smile on his lips as he fulfilled her every desire. A soft sigh escaped her as she thought about the delights he could bring her, the things he could do to make her hum with pleasure.

Cook, clean, and fetch the remote control.

Ah, yes. Men could have their uses, if only they'd cooperate.

"Laura?" She pried her eyes open just in time to see him lean closer, and outrage filled her with some extra energy when she realised he was trying to smell her breath.

"I'm not drunk!" she protested, pushing herself away from the wall, straight into him. His arm went over her shoulder as if to keep her from falling and her face got squashed against his chest.

Oh, no. Now would not be a good time to take a breath, she reminded herself, just as her lungs decided the opposite. Too much proximity to Justin was not a good thing. It just made her wonder what it would be like to hitch a ride on his motorcycle—despite her motorcycle phobia.

She pushed herself away, inhaled, grabbed her briefcase and squirmed past him with determined moves. The next flight of stairs taunted her. They were steep. They were long. But she could conquer them.

"Don't worry about me," she said over her shoulder to Justin, who was standing there with his hands on his hips, hovering over her. "I'm just exhausted. Some of us don't have the luxury of a forty-hour week, you know!" She didn't know precisely what Justin did for a living, how true the "teacher" rumor was—but he was always home before she was. He never seemed to work weekends, either.

Envy was a powerful thing. If she was honest with herself, his lack of overtime was probably the prime reason she resented him. That, and the home-cooked pizzas. She hardly knew him, so there wasn't any real, logical reason, but she told herself that it was because of his arrogance. Men who rode flashy motorcycles were always too arrogant for their own good.

Of course, if she dug deeper, which she wasn't necessarily interested in doing, she might find that the real reason was that he hadn't shown the slightest bit of interest in her during the six months they'd been living side by side. Some friendly neighborly chat when they met on the stairs, yes, some fascinating ten-second discussions about the weather and the state of the front yard, but that was it.

She turned her head to look at him, and sent him a glare to match his own stare. Yep, she was definitely peeved. Not that she was actually interested, despite that silly crush. He wasn't her type, even if she had time for irrelevant things like the mandatory search for a soul mate, true love and happily ever after. It was just a matter of pride. It wouldn't kill him to send her a flirty smile every now and then.

"That's some exhaustion," Justin remarked, following on her heels as she plodded up a few steps. "You're dead on your feet. Are you sure you're not sick?"

"Yeah, I'm fine. I'm just tired. And hungry. It's my own fault. I spent my lunch hour—not that it's actually an hour, more like ten minutes—buying underwear. So I haven't eaten anything since this morning." She frowned in thought, and didn't really care she was rambling. "No wait, I guess I haven't eaten at all since yesterday. There wasn't anything edible in the kitchen this morning. I was going to get a sandwich somewhere, but then I was too busy all day."

"You bought underwear instead of eating. I see." He stepped up beside her and looked her over. "You're scrawny. I could easily carry you upstairs."

Carry her upstairs?

Fantasy was one thing, reality was something else altogether. "I'm not an invalid," she grumbled and grabbed the banister, hauling herself up one more step. Scrawny? That put her in her place. Why couldn't he have said thin? Slim? Slender? All those were positive, alluring, sexy. Scrawny, on the other hand, was not sexy. It conjured up images of famine victims or stray cats, and she wasn't quite that far gone. Yet.

So that was it. He liked his women voluptuous. No wonder she hadn't received any of those sexy smiles. "I can make it," she grumbled, and conquered another step, just to show him.

"At least let me carry your briefcase for you. It looks heavy."

"Okay. Thanks," she added grudgingly, as she handed him her black leather briefcase. It had been brand-new when she started at the firm, but it wasn't surprising that it was already showing signs of wear. "Be careful, though. The weight of the world is in there."

It did indeed feel like the weight of the world was in her briefcase. She wasn't quite sure how a rookie like herself ended up assigned to all the difficult custody cases the firm handled, but they were interfering with her sleep and her peace of mind, and she badly needed both. In many cases, these were no-win situations, with the children as the biggest victims.

Sometimes she really hated her dream job.

Justin took her briefcase, and for a second, she actually felt better. Step by step, she made it to the second floor, with Justin following quietly. Fatigue returned with a vengeance then, and she slid down to sit on the top step, desperate for just a few minutes to gather her strength. She rested her head on her knees and groaned, embarrassed to be showing such weakness in front of Justin. But she really was running on empty. "I'll just rest for a minute, Justin. If you go on up ahead and leave the briefcase by my front door, that'll be great."

A curse exploded out of Justin's mouth. He leaned over her, dumped the briefcase in her arms and scooped her up. She opened her mouth to protest and stiffened in an effort to get out of his arms, but he had carried her the rest of the way before she could even get a word out. "Yes, definitely scrawny," he repeated under his breath. "You weigh next to nothing. No wonder you have no energy."

Laura would have protested, but she couldn't. Mostly because the body contact jolted all air out of her, and replaced it with liquid fire at being pressed against him. He smelled far, far too good.

Starvation did funny things to your body chemistry.

"Keys," he barked, as he was standing at her front door, not even breathing hard from the exertion. He wasn't looking like he would be putting her down any time soon, either. "What are you trying to do to yourself, Laura? You have to know your own limits or you'll make yourself sick."

Mr. Protective, wasn't he? Should she be calling him Mr. Mom? "Let me down," she mumbled into his neck. Later, she'd be indignant over his interference. Right now, she was too busy being mortified over the surge of lust that had assailed her as soon as he'd taken her into his arms. The things exhaustion and hunger did to your brain. Short-circuited all the sensible centers and made you lust after men you had no business—or time—to lust after.

He was warm. Solid. Still smelled of leather, even though he wasn't wearing his jacket anymore. What she really wanted to do was to put her arms around his neck and cuddle closer, preferably fall asleep right there, and then, when she woke up, things could get interesting.

There was no denying it. Her latent crush on her neighbor, almost forgotten in the hectic first months of her new job, had resurfaced in full force.

"Well?" Justin asked impatiently.

She surfaced from her rumination to realize he still hadn't put her down. She squirmed a bit, but stopped since it just reminded her tired body of where it was and with whom. "Justin, let me down. My keys are in the briefcase, I need to get them out."

A sense of loss ambushed her when he did as she asked, dropped her to her feet and stepped away. She cursed herself as she got her keys from the briefcase.

Home, sweet home, just inches away. She should be thinking of the comfort of her home, not the comfort of Justin's arms. She should be thinking of sliding under the covers of her bed—alone.

As the key finally slid into the lock—it only took four attempts—she looked up at him and tried for a smile. She was too tired for a confrontation over his bossy behavior. And he'd meant well, probably. Actually, she realized, he hadn't done anything wrong. It wasn't his fault there was a voice screaming inside her head, telling her to grab the front of his shirt and yank him inside with her. "Thanks for your help, Justin. I would have made it up here by myself eventually, but thanks, anyway."

He grabbed her arm, preventing her from entering her apartment. "Is there someone you can call? Someone to stay with you? You don't seem to be in any condition to be alone right now."

"I'll be fine. Really, there's no need to worry about me. Thanks." She slipped her arm from his grasp and escaped inside, shutting the door behind her. The briefcase fell forgotten to the floor as she leaned against the door, eyes closed. After a moment she heard Justin's footsteps retreat, and then the sound of his own door closing.

She contemplated just dropping down on the floor for a nap instead of trying anything more ambitious tonight. The instruments of torture known as high-heeled shoes continued to squeeze her feet, and her shirt stuck to her back. She needed a shower, a change of clothes, food and sleep, in that order, but right now, a weekend spent curled up right there on tiles that hadn't seen soap and water in too many weeks didn't sound too bad.

Two seconds later adrenaline flooded her system, abolishing the exhaustion as surely as a whole weekend of sleep.

There was someone inside her apartment.

Laura snatched the briefcase up off the floor and held it in front of her as a shiny leather shield, standing immobile in a defensive posture as she stared in the direction of the sound.

The noise had come from her bedroom. Heart racing, she tiptoed closer—no mean feat in those shoes—and stuck her head out into the open space between the living room, the bedroom and the entrance. She couldn't see anything. The bedroom door was half-closed.

She held herself still, trying to think despite the panic. Had she left that door half-closed this morning? Her head started to hurt as she tried to dig up details of the hectic morning. She couldn't remember. Barely breathing, she looked in the other direction, toward the living room. Nothing out of the ordinary there. Nothing seemed to have been taken.

But she'd definitely heard something.

She couldn't hear anything now, but that might be due to the blood pounding in her ears, a combination of fear and rage, bludgeoning its way through the numbing exhaustion. She was a private person; the thought of someone entering her home without permission, rummaging through her belongings, was abhorrent, more horrible than the thought of them actually stealing her few valuables.

Fear and rage battled for a few moments, and fear won. It made no sense to confront the burglars. She should escape while she could, call the police from a neighbor's apartment, and let them deal with it, even if it meant that the thugs would have time to get away. There was no other choice. Under normal circumstances she wouldn't stand a chance of overpowering a man on her own, and in her current condition, probably not even if he actively cooperated.

Still clutching her leather shield, Laura had almost backed all the way out the front door, when she heard the low sound coming from her bedroom a second time. She paused, listening hard. The noise was difficult to define. It wasn't anything breaking, not a grunt from someone trying to lift her computer out of the window, not a voice, not even footsteps. Just a…sound.

She hesitated, remembering the last time she'd thought there was a burglar in the place. She'd shot out of there and attacked Justin's door screaming until he had opened it, then wrapped herself around him, trembling and stuttering, overcome with terror. At the time he'd just moved in next door, and as first impressions went, this one must have been…unique.

He'd been nice, she grudgingly admitted. Patronizing, yes, but helpful and polite. He'd managed to disentangle her from his body with the lure of offering her a calming cup of coffee, and after he'd finally managed to decode her incoherent stutters, he'd led her to the phone. He'd even pushed the buttons for her when her fingers shook too hard to press 9-1-1. Of course, as a typical male, he'd wanted to check out the situation himself, but she'd grabbed hold of him again and refused to let him leave.

The police had arrived, although they took long enough for her to get comfortably stuck in the role of "hysterical female" in the eyes of her new neighbor. The policemen had entered the apartment, badges gleaming, guns at ready, machismo in motion, and after a brief search removed the offender. Uncuffed.

The villain turned out to be a gorgeous white kitten with a nametag that said Angel, still washing her face as she rested snug in the arms of the policeman, purring her catty little heart out. The damage was minimal: she'd dug Laura's leftover tuna sandwich out of the garbage and had a little feast on the kitchen floor. Nothing a mop wouldn't fix. And nothing seemed to be missing, the two policemen had informed her with identical smirks on their faces, and added that they'd be sure to book and pawprint the perpetrator before returning her to her family.

Justin, leaning against his doorjamb with arms crossed on his chest as he watched the show, seemed to enjoy this part of the action. He'd shared a knowing grin with the cops. None of them actually said it out loud, but Laura could almost hear them mutter "women" in a tone that should have gone out with black and white television.

She bit her lip and reconsidered her options. Nope, a repeat performance of her woman-in-jeopardy act was not the solution.

There was a sound from the bedroom for the third time. Not anything breaking, not the rough voices of thugs with panty hose on their heads complaining about a nylon allergy. Just a soft sound that could very well come from a cat.

To make sure she had an escape route, Laura opened the front door wide, and propped it in place with a shoe. She backed all the way out of the apartment and stood fidgeting, wondering what to do. Check out the situation herself? Or call the police, after all? She'd have to borrow a neighbor's phone for that. There was only one phone in her apartment, and it was in the bedroom.

She swore to buy a cell phone first thing tomorrow. Sometimes it seemed she was the only person on the planet without one.

"Everything okay?" Justin was at his door, arms crossed and a rather suspicious look on his face as he stared at her with narrowed eyes. "What's wrong?"

He did not deserve those good looks, she thought, not for the first time. In fact, it was quite irritating, the way she almost felt compelled to sigh in admiration every time she got a look at that chiseled face and the wavy brown hair that looked even softer than hair in conditioner commercials.

And his eyes... Nope, she wouldn't even go there. She didn't want to think about his eyes. Thankfully she didn't often see them up close. Those dark eyes framed by mile-long lashes reminded her of chocolate, and everybody knew chocolate was a sinful sensual indulgence. They could distract you even when there was potentially a homicidal maniac inside her apartment.

Definitely not good for you.

Justin shook his head and walked closer. "You're white as a sheet. And you're not talking. What's up?"

Laura stared into chocolate-brown eyes as he approached. Yep. Delicious. His brow was creased in worry, but there was also a tiny smile on his lips, and she drew her brows together in a frown, trying to decode it. Was this a friendly neighbor smile, or a "women!" smirk? Was he remembering a hysterical woman with her arms wrapped around his neck, shrieking panicked nothings in his ear, doing a "helpless female" imitation like something from the eighteenth century?

Justin stopped right in front of her. "Laura, are you sure you're not sick? I should call a doctor."

Her spine stiffened and she straightened, giving him an excellent facsimile of a carefree smile. The corners of her lips almost moved and all. "No, thank you, everything's fine." He didn't move away, so she turned back to her apartment. "Really, I'm fine. Thanks for your concern."

Justin's gaze searched her face. He didn't look happy, but shrugged and turned around, vanishing inside his own apartment and leaving Laura alone with her predicament. She didn't want to admit it, but she felt a bit better, knowing her neighbor was home. All she had to do was scream, and he'd hear it through the thin walls.

She took a determined step forward ending up on the right side of the wide open door.

Of course it wasn't a burglar, she soothed herself. Why was she so quick to panic? She'd probably left her bedroom window open again, and Angel had decided to check if tuna was still on the menu. The cat lived somewhere close by; those green eyes and white whiskers made a regular appearance in the street. So far, Laura's withering glares had seemed to have done the intended job of letting the cat know she was less than welcome on a repeat visit. But perhaps the temptation of tuna had been too much for the creature.

She wouldn't again let a curious cat chase her into Justin's arms. She would march in there and chase the cat out of there herself. This time, Angel could be the one seeking shelter with Justin.

Grabbing an umbrella, just in case the trespasser was more menacing than the furry little beast, she double-checked that the front door was still open as an escape—

either for herself or for the cat—and crept toward the bedroom. The door was half-closed, and a slight draft confirmed her suspicions of having left the window open.

Muscles tense and both hands clutching the umbrella, she peeked inside the room. Everything looked just as she'd left it, the afternoon sun illuminating the dusty surfaces all too well: the rumpled bed she hadn't made, the overflowing bookcase and the overturned crate that served as her night table.

No burglar. And no cat.

She left the umbrella against the wall, straightened up and pushed the door fully open. All this for nothing. That sound she'd heard must have been something from outside, or maybe the window creaking.

She stalked inside the room and sat down on the bed. That was that. Just as well she hadn't panicked. Much.

Sitting down had been a mistake, she realized. Now she'd have to stand up again, if only to close the front door. She sighed, postponing the ordeal, and idly contemplated the upturned crate with its miniature mountain of books and paper. Okay, it was high time to get a proper nightstand. She could afford it. She could afford a lot of things now, and it was time to stop worrying about every dime.

Then something moved just behind her on the bed and before she'd even acknowledged the movement she was standing pressed against the wall, not realizing she was screaming until her throat hurt and the screeching sound echoed off the wall and exploded in her own ears.

Justin grabbed a dish of leftover pizza out of the fridge and put it in the microwave. Irritation was making him edgy, and he wasn't sure why he was reheating pizza right now. He wasn't even hungry.

His neighbor needed a baby-sitter. She practically lived at her office, dragged herself home late at night looking like a ghost on a hunger strike, and when at home she didn't seem to do much more than sleep. There was hardly ever a sound from her place, even through the thin wall.

Except when she showered. Her bathroom was just on the other side of his shower tiles. She took long showers. They sometimes coincided with his. In his weaker moments, he stood there in his own shower and lived every moment of hers. He had this crazy urge to wash that long brown hair for her. Maybe this was what they called a fetish. Maybe he was a shampoo-and-conditioner fetishist.

She was also thin, and getting thinner. No wonder, if she used her breaks to shop for clothing, instead of eating.

Women!

He stared at the pizza, turning in slow circles inside the humming microwave. It would be neighborly to bring over some food, wouldn't it? Wasn't it the gesture of a friendly old lady, living next door, concerned for the welfare of her neighbor? It wouldn't smack of a secret admirer who'd spent too many hours listening to her shower, would it?

He grimaced at himself, as familiar visions of soap-suds and glistening skin intruded on his altruistic thoughts. In the last few months he'd come up with ideas for all sorts of interesting things to do with a washcloth.

He'd have to adjust his fantasies, though. The way

she was losing weight, he could probably occupy himself in the shower by counting her ribs.

Justin cursed himself and yanked the microwave door open, three seconds before it was due to stop. Laura was not his type. There was vulnerability in her eyes that marked her strictly off limits to someone like him. He wasn't a saint, but he tried not to get involved with women who expected more than he would ever want to give.

He'd just take her the damn pizza, and be done with it.

He was at the door when the scream ricocheted through the building. Adrenaline pounding through his body, he yanked the baseball bat from the umbrella stand, and half a second later was at Laura's door.

CHAPTER TWO

IT'S just the cat, just the cat, someone chanted in her ear and she realized it was herself. She forced herself to look at the bed, expecting the white Angel to be sitting there, looking accusatory over the lack of tuna.

But no.

Laura blinked when the shape on the bed took form. It wasn't a cat. It was bigger than a cat, not as furry, and probably wasn't obliging enough to lick itself clean.

A baby.

She squeezed her eyes shut and counted to twenty before opening them again. Maybe stress had caught up with her. After all, she'd been working fourteen hours a day for almost two weeks now. Yes, it had to be stress. Stress working with her biological clock to create the illusion of a tiny baby sleeping in her bed. Her biological clock had probably been awakened by the unusual stimulus of a real life male in close proximity. The child had to be an illusion. For one, if it had been a real baby, it would have woken up when she screamed.

Yes. That was it. It had to be an illusion. She opened her eyes, feeling better already.

The illusion was still there.

Still sleeping. Looking very, very real, tiny nose, chubby cheeks, long lashes and all. The soft baby-snore convinced her that the infant was for real.

Illusions didn't snore.

How could there be a baby lying in the middle of her

bed? In her locked apartment? She pinched herself. If it wasn't an illusion, perhaps it was a dream?

Nope. No such luck.

"Laura?"

Mr. Chocolate Eyes again, his voice also chocolate smooth as it snaked through the small apartment, even raised in urgent inquiry. She groaned. He must have heard her scream, and, ever gallant, come to the rescue.

"Laura?" he called again. "I heard you scream, and the door is open. I'm coming in, okay? I'm calling the police."

She shot to her feet and out in the hallway, just as Justin barged into the apartment, body tensed for fight, cell phone in one hand, a baseball bat in the other.

"I'm fine," she said, trying for a smile. "No need for the police. There's no danger. I was just startled. Sorry if I scared you."

His eyebrow rose. "The scream turned my blood to ice. What was it?"

Laura tugged at her hair, not sure herself what was going on. "There's nothing wrong." Exactly. There was just a strange baby lying in her bed.

"Do we have another cat burglar?"

"Haha," she said dutifully, grinding her teeth at the reminder. "Yes. I mean, no. Not precisely."

"Dog burglar?"

"Well, since you ask, it's actually a baby burglar. Did you see anyone around today?"

"No, I just got home the same time as you did." Justin slid his cell phone into his pocket. "Baby burglar? What are you talking about?"

"Someone left a baby in my apartment."

"I see." He left the baseball bat leaning against the

wall. "Guess I won't be needing that. You mean you're baby-sitting?"

"Apparently. Only I have no idea whose baby it is. Come see." Without giving him the chance to decline, she turned toward her bedroom again, relieved to hear him follow. This was too much to handle alone.

"See?" She moved around to the other side of the bed to give him an unobstructed view. She pointed at the evidence. "A baby. He was just lying there when I got home."

Justin stared down at the sleeping intruder. "I see," he repeated.

"Well, what do you think?" she asked impatiently, when he didn't seem about to elaborate.

He looked at her with a crooked smile. "Well, your diagnosis is correct. It is a baby."

"Are you always this patronizing, or is it something I bring out in you?"

He didn't answer, but bent over the child for a closer look. "He's okay, isn't he?" he asked. "Just sleeping, not unconscious or anything?"

"How should I know? He was just lying there when I got home," she said. Shock was dissipating and confusion settling in instead. "He looks fine, he's breathing fine and everything. And he was making some sounds before." Scaring the wits out of her, just like Angel had.

She slid down to sit on the edge of the bed, not taking her eyes off the child for one second. Despite the way she had screamed, the infant was fast asleep, both hands up above his head, as he nearly vanished into the soft duvet. If he'd been closer to the edge she could have sat down on him, she thought in horror. His hair was coal black and slightly curly. The tiny fists were curled, half inside the sleeves of his sweater.

All in all, a pretty adorable kid, if you were the motherly type. He was dressed in a green and white sweater, green overalls and white socks, a green pacifier hanging from a clip. In one fist he was clutching a green teething ring.

We have our first clue, Laura's hysterical side interjected quite cheerfully, as she reached out and tentatively touched a green garment. This baby must be Irish.

Okay. She had to stop panicking and start thinking. What was this baby doing here? Thank God he was asleep. She didn't have a clue about babies. Her experience was more or less limited to having been one, once upon a long ago, and she didn't think that would be much help.

Think. Whose baby could this be? Why was he there? She did not know this baby. She didn't know a lot of babies, and none of them had keys to her apartment.

"Who is he?"

Laura started. She'd almost forgotten Justin was here. "I told you, I have no idea who he is. I don't know anyone with an infant. Heck, I don't even know any heavily pregnant women. Do you suppose he's a newborn?"

"I have no idea. It's been a while since I've been around babies."

She cocked her head to the side as she checked the child's size. "I'd guess he was a few months old. He looks far too big to give birth to. Of course, they always do."

"Yeah, well, nature knows what she's doing."

"Easy for you to say. Nature didn't give you a uterus and forget to include the zipper."

He looked at her across the bed, frowning. "Do you have some sort of a childbirth phobia?"

Laura brought her fingers to her temples, trying to keep her voice a whisper in the hope that the child would stay asleep until this nightmare ended. "Listen to us, we're both babbling. What do I do about the kid? I can't believe this is happening to me."

Justin shrugged. "I'm sure the kid won't be any more happy about it than you are, when he wakes up. Are you sure you don't know his parents? Why would someone leave him here of all places? And how did they get in? Does someone have a key?"

"I don't know his parents! And I don't know how they got in. It's possible that I left the window open."

Justin straightened up and crossed to the window. He leaned out to examine the frame. "No, you didn't. It's been forced open."

"I told you, a baby burglar," Laura said. She felt hysterics emerge from within and head for the surface. No. Not again. She'd be calm and efficient, and do what needed to be done—call the police.

And she would not wrap herself around Justin like a princess who'd finally located her knight in shining armor, never mind how good he looked in his leather jacket. "I thought this was a safe neighborhood."

"It is."

"Right. I feel so safe now, knowing that anyone can just climb the fire escape and use a crowbar to force their way into my bedroom."

"There's something out here," Justin muttered, still

at the window, but she was too preoccupied to pay much attention.

She reached for the phone on the bedside table. "I'll call the police."

Justin was beside her in a flash, and the weight of his hand descended on hers, stopping her from grabbing the phone. "Wait. Don't call the police yet."

"Why not?"

"We don't know what's going on here. If you call the police, that kid will be in foster care before you know it. If this is a friend's child, or some sort of a misunderstanding or a mistake, it will be hell for the parents to get him back. They might not get him back at all."

"Well, if they leave their child like this, they damn well deserve to go a few rounds with the authorities! Anything could have happened to him while he was alone here."

"He wasn't alone." Justin was looking toward the window. "See?" He pointed.

Out on the fire escape there was a small green tote bag.

"His mother or father probably waited out there for you to come home, making sure he would be safe."

"Maybe there's some explanation in that bag."

Justin crossed the room to the window and leaned out for the bag. Laura jumped to her feet just as Justin picked it up. "Don't! There might be fingerprints!"

He wasn't listening, but unzipped the bag, and rummaged inside. "There's a note."

"Wait!" Laura dashed to the bathroom and fetched tweezers. Law school did have its uses. She ran back and picked up the note from where it was wedged in between baby clothing. It was lined paper, ripped out of a notebook. Empty on one side, six words scrawled in green ink on the other side: *Good luck, will be in touch.*

"What sort of a note is that?" Disappointed, Laura let the note drop to the nightstand-crate.

"Sounds like a note from someone who knows you and is trusting you with her baby."

"I don't know this baby," Laura repeated for what seemed like the millionth time.

Justin upended the bag on an empty spot on her bed. There wasn't much in it, just clothes and mainly undergarments. He went through the pile, meticulously looking at each item before putting it back into the bag.

"Well, we know two things about the mother. The clothes are good quality, so she's not lacking in money. And she's a tree hugger."

"How do you know?"

Justin lifted a pile of white things. "Environmentally friendly diapers. She doesn't use disposables for her son."

Not only a baby, but a baby with old-fashioned diapers. Suddenly the problem had multiplied. Laura backed away. "You mean the kind you wash instead of stuffing in a bag and throwing away?"

"Yep."

Yuck. "That's it. I'm calling the police."

"Because of washable diapers?"

"That was the last straw, yes."

Justin let the diapers fall back to the bed. "You can't do that, Laura. Someone trusts you to look after her baby. Someone who may be in trouble. You can't betray their trust and give their baby to Social Services."

"Why do you talk about Social Services as if I'm delivering the baby to total doom? They are there to protect children.''

''I know. And they do, the best they can, when there is no one else there for the child. But now there is some-one else.''

''There is? Who?''

Justin rolled his eyes. ''You. The person the parents trusted with their baby.''

''I don't know this baby.''

Justin shrugged. ''His mother or father could be an old friend perhaps? You must have some friends you haven't seen in a few months, maybe even a year or two?''

''Well, yes...'' She slid down to sit on the bed. A small fist waved in the air as the baby's dream was dis-turbed, but he settled down again and Laura allowed herself to breathe. A few more minutes of peace, that was all they had. He had to wake up any minute now. ''Of course. I've been so busy lately that I've almost lost touch with even my closest friends. Then there are friends from college, from my summer jobs. High school friends. But I can't believe any of them would dump their infant baby on me without a word.'' She stood, careful not to disturb the baby again. ''Let's talk in the living room, where we don't disturb him.''

Justin followed her, bumping into her back when she stopped short at the sight of her living room.

''Oh, damn.''

Justin put his hand on his shoulder and pushed her to the side. ''Wait here, I'll go first. Looks like it was a burglar after all.''

How embarrassing. ''No...this is how it usually looks these days.''

His look was incredulous, and embarrassment made her lash out at him.

"Well, maybe you're the perfect housewife, Justin, but I'm not. I'm swamped with work. I was so exhausted that I didn't think I'd make it up the stairs! I don't know how this happened…but things just pile up and then all of a sudden it's Messville. Ordinarily I'm not a slob. So don't judge me."

"Hey, what did I say?"

"Nothing. But you've got expressive eyes."

Eyes she'd made the mistake of looking into from close up. Hypnotizing. A woman would throw away her map and happily get lost in there for days.

Justin gestured to the sofa. "Can we move the…stuff away and sit down?"

"Sure." She grabbed an armful of papers and books and dumped it on top of the diminishing mountain of clean laundry on the coffee table. At least she knew for a fact there wasn't any underwear there. "There. Have a seat."

He did. "Do you know any tree huggers?"

Laura dropped down by his side, fatigue seeping into her bones again now that the adrenaline was getting the picture: no one to fight or flee, just diapers to change. Probably not an event worthy of a full-scale hormonal attack. "I know a lot of environmentally conscious people, yes. People who are into recycling and conserving the rain forests."

"Good. That narrows it down."

"Are you suggesting I take my phone book and call all the recyclers in there and ask if they'd happened to drop a baby off in my apartment today?"

"We could also just wait for the mother to call."

"Or the father. Or both. We don't know who left him here."

"That's true."

Her head fell back against the sofa. "The right thing to do is to call the police. We don't know the story. He might have been mistreated for all we know."

"He seems to be well cared for. Even his clothes are color-coordinated."

Laura shook her head. "I can't, Justin. Even if I wanted to…" She shook her head again. "It's illegal. If the parents don't come for the child and we have to bring in the police I could be disbarred."

"I'll take responsibility."

"What?"

He made an impatient gesture. "The baby was found in my apartment. It was my decision to wait for the parents to contact me."

"Lying to the police?"

"Adjusting the truth microscopically."

She narrowed her eyes. "Are you a lawyer, too?"

He chuckled. "No."

"What is it you do, by the way? Mrs. Carlson upstairs talks about you as 'our resident teacher.' Any truth in that, or is it just her nerve pills speaking?"

"She's right. I have a teaching diploma, but I mostly work as a speech therapist."

Speech therapist. Of all the occupations in the world, she wouldn't have guessed that one in a million years. It didn't go with the motorbike. She made a mental note to pry further later. "Why is this so important to you?"

"I know what foster care can be like. I don't wish it on an infant."

There was obviously a story behind that statement, delivered in a clipped tone devoid of emotion.

"I'm sorry you had a bad experience, but foster care is often excellent, handled by caring, loving people."

"Yes. And sometimes it's not."

"Be reasonable, Justin. You don't know who left him here and why. His parents may be searching for him. If we don't turn him in, that's kidnapping. He'll be well looked after by the authorities."

"This is a tiny baby, just a few months old. He needs care. He needs bonding. Do you know what happens to infants who don't bond with a caretaker in the first few months? They may never recover."

"He'll get good care. He'll get better care, better bonding, with someone who knows what they're doing." She gestured at the two of them. "And neither of us does. Neither of us has even the time to look after a baby."

"We're capable. I've got the time, and I want to help."

"So you just want to take this baby?"

Justin's sigh suggested she was being extremely difficult. "I'm not suggesting we steal him, Laura. Just that we look after him while we try to track down his parents. There has to be a reason he was left here. We'll figure it out and find his parents."

"And then what? We give him back to people who left him alone on a strange doorstep?"

"I don't know. We don't know the circumstances. We'll deal with that when the time comes."

She shook her head. "Justin, you're not thinking clearly. The only logical thing to do is to turn this over to the police and Social Services. They know what to do.''

"Maybe. Maybe not. There are good people there, of course there are. Probably the majority. But there are no guarantees. He might also be neglected. He might be shuffled between places. He won't know the security of one caretaker, one home, while he's away from his folks. He'll be much better off with us until we can find his mother.''

"I don't know. I could really get in trouble. *We* could get in a lot of trouble." Laura groaned. Calling the police, Social Services, anyone who would deal with the situation was suddenly imperative.

"Obviously this is someone you know, Laura. Probably an old friend. And she said she'd be in touch. She'll probably call in a day or two, explain everything. Or come by and pick up the baby.''

"A day or two?" Frustrated, Laura bit her lip hard. "Do you have any idea how many diapers I'd have to change in a day or two?''

"No.''

"Me neither! I don't know anything about babies. It's for the best if we call the police. He'll be safe then.''

"Look." Justin looked grim and determined. "I'll help, okay? Between the two of us we should be fine.''

"But what if this baby has been kidnapped? We'd be accomplices to a felony. His mother could be searching for him right this minute.''

"We'd have heard on the news if there was a baby missing.''

"Not necessarily. Maybe he was kidnapped and the parents warned not to call the police.''

"And the kidnappers just randomly choose an apartment, one apartment in this complex, to keep him safe meanwhile? So in a few days they'll be knocking on your door asking you to return him so they can claim their ransom?''

She gritted her teeth. "Or, they are counting on us to return him through the police. So they won't get caught when returning him."

"Isn't that a rather far-fetched idea?"

Why did he have to sound so reasonable and she so hysterical? Those were stereotypical roles she did not approve of, and besides, she was making sense and he wasn't.

"It's not a big deal, Laura. If nobody is in touch in a day or two, then we'll go to the police, okay?"

There was a noise from the bedroom. Laura and Justin were at the door instantly. In the bed, the baby stirred. Laura held her breath and noticed Justin did the same, as the baby's eyes fluttered open, revealing dark blue eyes. The child looked at them, surprise widening his eyes. Any time now, Laura thought in resignation. He would open that rosebud mouth and start screaming for his mother.

The baby opened his mouth and laughed. He had two tiny teeth in his lower gum and used both of them to hack at Laura's heart.

Maybe he would be better off here with them after all. Just while they sorted out this mess with his parents.

"Looks like he's quite happy to be here," Justin said.

"We need diapers for him," Laura said, giving in, just for the time being. "That first diaper change will not be the old-fashioned way, rain forests or not."

"No argument from me."

"And then once we have some diapers, we actually have to change his diaper."

"We?" Justin stepped back. "Oh, no. I have to help with the diapers, too?"

Laura stared at him and sputtered. "This was your idea! You're expecting me to handle the dirty stuff? Are you nuts? If I had my way, that kid would already be in the hands of professional diaper changers. Either you're in, or I turn the kid in."

Justin's eyes narrowed at her tone. "Is this a joke to you?"

"Not even close. And we still have that diaper to change."

"I don't think I know how to."

"Well, not to worry. We're two fully competent professional adults. We can change a diaper. First things first: we need to buy some diapers."

"That's right." Justin looked relieved. "We need some diapers."

They were both at the front door when they noticed the other one was there, too.

"I'm going to buy the diapers," Laura stated firmly.

"No, I am. You're exhausted. Even if you make it to the store, you're in no shape to make it back up the stairs. You can stay here and rest with the baby."

Hah! Nice try. She could see the panic in his eyes. It wasn't concern for her that made him want to be the one to escape for half an hour. No. He was just as terrified at the thought of being left alone with the child as she was.

"I'm not staying here alone with him. I don't have a clue when it comes to infants. That wasn't covered in law school."

"How hard can it be? Just watch him, make sure he doesn't…do whatever it is babies can do to harm themselves."

Laura took a step forward, but he did, too, wedging them stuck in the open doorway.

Stalemate.

Laura gave up. "We'll both go and take him with us, okay?"

Laura had never before realized what a huge section of the supermarket was dedicated to babies and all their paraphernalia. Just the diaper racks seemed to stretch for miles. The selection was daunting. She'd never imagined all the factors that needed to be taken into account.

"How much does he weigh?" She peered at a diaper package. "More or less than six pounds, do you think?"

"More. Definitely more," Justin said darkly, adjusting the baby on his shoulder. He was still behaving, gurgling and smiling, and hadn't screamed once. It couldn't last. It was just a matter of time before he realized that there was something very wrong with the world. If he didn't realize it sooner, he most definitely would in a while, when he had two novices trying to change his diaper.

"Okay. More or less than fifteen pounds?"

Justin lifted the child up and hefted him experimentally. "Hmm…fifteen pounds sounds about right."

"That doesn't help. One package is for babies who weigh ten to fifteen pounds, the other for babies weighing fifteen to twenty pounds. So which is it?"

Without looking at the markings, Justin grabbed one of the packages out of her arms and tossed it in the cart. "This one."

Laura shrugged. "Fine."

"What more? We need bottles, don't we? And formula?"

"Definitely," Laura chirped. "Unless you're planning on breastfeeding him."

Three kinds of formula landed in the cart and he didn't even pretend to smile at her brilliant wit.

"What about baby food?" Justin asked, pointing at the opposite shelves. "That stuff in the jars? Do we need that?"

"I don't know when they start eating baby food. And we don't know how old he is."

"We'll just buy a few different jars, and see if he wants any of it, okay?" He didn't wait for an answer before moving the cart to the baby food section.

"Diapers, food. What else do babies need?"

She gnawed her lip. "Wet-wipes? Pacifiers? Special soap perhaps?"

"Sounds reasonable. A few toys, perhaps. And a teddy bear. There is a toy department around here somewhere."

"A teddy bear?"

He looked at her defensively. "Every kid needs a teddy bear. Especially when all on his own without his folks around."

"You're right." She grinned. "I still have mine, sitting on top of the bookshelf in the bedroom. He even has both his eyes, but his front paw is bandaged. Do you still have yours?"

"I didn't have one. We'll have to find a sturdy one for the baby."

"Yes." She held her arms out for the baby, and pointed to a shelf too high for her to reach. "Get that lotion, please. Also the big box of wet-wipes over there. And you're right, Patrick looks like an active boy. He'll need a strong and sturdy teddy.''

''Patrick? Why are you calling him Patrick?''

''Well, we have to call him something, don't we?''

Justin stopped in the middle of the aisle, wet-wipes in one hand, lotion in the other. He stared at her with a look of warning. ''Laura, don't get attached to this baby.''

''You're warning *me* not to get attached? You're the one who wants to risk imprisonment and a criminal record just to keep him with us.''

''Shh!'' Justin hissed, looking around to see if anyone had heard her. ''Are you trying to get us arrested? At least I'm not giving him a name.''

Laura's arms tightened around Patrick. ''I refuse to call him 'baby.' It dehumanizes him.''

Justin shrugged, tossing the boxes into the cart. ''Okay. We'll call him Patrick. Why Patrick, anyway?''

''He looks Irish. All this clothes are green.''

''Irrefutable logic,'' he remarked dryly.

Patrick finally started crying on the way home. It wasn't surprising, after all, the poor little guy hadn't been changed, and hadn't gotten anything to eat or drink since he'd woken up.

''Maybe we should go to my apartment,'' Justin suggested, turning to the right without waiting for her to agree. ''It's not as... There's more...room there.''

Laura rolled her eyes. ''You mean less mess.''

''That, too.''

''I know, I live in a pigsty,'' Laura sighed. ''I've been

working fourteen-hour days. I need a wife. I even had to go without underwear this morning.''

Justin looked back at her and she blushed. ''I'm wearing underwear now!'' she stated. ''I already told you, I bought some during my lunch break.''

''Right.''

Great. Now she had her hunky, baby-loving neighbor imagining her naked under her prim working suit. She disguised her mortification by looking around Justin's apartment. It was a mirror of her own, but a lot neater than her own place had been in months. Yes, he had definite potential as a housekeeper.

There was large microwave container sitting on a small stool by the front door. She raised an eyebrow. ''Takeout?''

Justin followed her gaze and shrugged. She even thought he looked a bit embarrassed. ''I was going to take it to you, when you screamed. You looked hungry.''

''You were going to bring me food?'' Laura was touched. Something tearlike even made it to her eyes and she blinked, blaming it on exhaustion. ''Justin, that's so nice of you.''

''Yeah, well, you still haven't eaten, have you? It's cold by now, but if you still want it, we can reheat it.'' He grabbed the container and made his way into the kitchen. ''It's not like it's anything fancy,'' he warned over his shoulder. ''Just leftover pizza.''

''Homemade?'' she breathed.

''Well, yes. How did you know?''

She dodged the question, not wanting to explain to him the way her nose had been picking up the wonderful scents from his kitchen for months now. ''First things first, a bottle for the little one.'' She looked at the child, squirming on Justin's shoulder. "He's really hungry. I'll get the bottle, if you take care of him in the meantime. Where do you keep your kettle?"

"It's right there on the countertop. We'll be in the living room."

She measured the formula carefully and before too long had a full bottle of warm white liquid. She tested the temperature and erred on the side of too cold, then hurried into the living room where Justin was busy being unsuccessful at calming baby Patrick down. "Here."

Justin passed her the baby. "Feed him. I'll go warm up the pizza for you."

Patrick gulped down the milk, making Laura feel terribly guilty. The poor baby must have been starving.

"Here. Eat this." Justin put a plate on the table, filled with the most delicious pizza Laura had ever seen, topped with enough cheese to fulfill her calcium requirements for a month. He'd brought a huge glass of milk, too. She raised an eyebrow. "Milk? With pizza?"

"It's good for you. Give me the kid, and feed yourself."

Smiling at his gruff tone, Laura handed him the child and started work on the pizza. Ravenous, she managed to finish before Patrick finished his bottle. But as soon as the bottle was empty he was crying again, and showed no interest in a second helping.

"Okay, diaper time. He's probably wet, too. Or worse." Laura felt more awake after her meal, and a lot stronger. Taking charge, she grabbed the baby out of Justin's arms. Women had been handling babies since the beginning of mankind. She had to have some kind of instincts on how to do this. "Can you get some towels to lay him on?"

Before long, the baby was lying on the floor on top of two thick towels and they were getting ready to take that diaper off. It was a cloth diaper, wet and heavy. With a grimace Laura removed it from the baby's sticky bottom and dumped it in the bag that Justin held ready. That was one diaper that wouldn't be washed.

She was reaching for the wet wipes when she noticed Justin staring down with a funny look on his face.

"What? What's wrong?" she asked, even as she followed his gaze and gasped at what she didn't see.

"Isn't there a little something missing?" Justin asked dryly.

CHAPTER THREE

"HE'S a girl!" Laura exclaimed.

Justin snorted. "You get top marks for observation skills, Laura. Why did you think she was a boy?"

"I just assumed she was a boy when I first saw her." Laura shrugged, staring at "Patrick's" face. "She looked like a boy to me. I don't know. It didn't even occur to me that she might be a girl."

The little lady's face scrunched up at this news, and she started crying again. Justin patted her cheek. "There, there," he soothed the child. "She didn't mean it. A dress and a bow in your hair and you'll be as feminine as they get. We'll get you something pink, promise." He looked at Laura, gesturing at the baby. "Now that I look at her, it seems obvious that she's a girl. Those eyes and the long lashes. Obviously a girl."

"Exactly! Her eyes are the kind reserved for boys, who don't appreciate them and spend most of their adolescence wondering if they can trim their lashes." She pointed at him. "You're a case in point."

Justin blinked. "I trimmed my lashes?"

"I don't know about that. But you do have gorgeous eyes."

Justin looked at her with something unreadable in those dark eyes until she was biting the inside of her cheeks in an effort to keep from blurting out something no doubt as stupid as her last remark. "Uh, thank you," he said at last and she hurried to change the subject.

"You're welcome. Now, can we go back to the diaper business?"

"Sure."

Laura rolled up her sleeves and turned her teeth on her lower lip in punishment for having actually gushed over the man's looks to his face.

Especially the same day he'd called her scrawny.

But there was no time to wallow in bruised pride. There was important work ahead. A diaper had been removed and another one—this one not out of the middle ages—had to be installed in its place.

Procrastinating a minute, she lined up the wet-wipes and lotions, which was tricky since they needed to be within her reach, but out of Patrick's…Pat's reach. Then she got to work at washing and drying a bottom that was slightly pink.

"Darn it," she muttered, feeling guilty. The new diaper was obviously long overdue. "She has a rash. I hope those lotions fix it. Poor thing." She picked up the three bottles and examined the instructions. "Hey, we can choose between instructions in French, Spanish and Japanese."

"There's English on the other side," Justin pointed out, and sure enough, there were four long paragraphs of small print, which effectively said: "Put lotion on baby's red bottom."

"This stuff better work," she muttered. The lotions had certainly been expensive enough, and Justin had insisted on buying three kinds: one for bad rashes, one for mild rashes, and one preventive.

Which one to choose? She peered at the red skin, but found no hidden message there.

"Is that a mild or a bad rash?" she wondered aloud.

Justin shrugged. "I have no idea."

"So what kind of lotion do we use? We've got three kinds."

Justin was looking blank, and worse, he was looking as if he expected her to know these things. Laura rolled her eyes and gave up on him. The next diaper he would handle on his own, she promised herself and turned her attention back to the baby.

At least Pat didn't seem to be in any discomfort yet from the mild or bad rash. And she was quite a kicker. Justin was sitting cross-legged by her head, distracting her by making funny faces, and the child kept kicking as she babbled and stretched her hands upward toward his face.

"Boy am I glad she's not crawling yet," Laura muttered, deciding to smooth on a mixture of all three lotions, as well as she could with two small feet trying to kick her hands away. "We'd never be able to keep up with her." She finished her work and sat up straight to dry the excess lotion off her fingers with a paper towel. "Okay, she's not going to get any more clean or moisturized. We're all set for stage two: a new diaper. Are you ready with one?"

"Wait." Justin had the unopened package of diapers in his hand, and was staring at it with an expression that suggested a roadblock ahead. "Problem."

Laura groaned. "What now? Instructions in Sanskrit?"

"Blue package."

"What has the color got to do with anything?"

"We bought boy diapers."

"Oh."

They stared at the girl who was not a boy.

"Don't you think it'll be okay for her to wear a boy diaper?" Laura asked. Would that cause irreparable psychological damage to the girl, above what she'd already had to suffer—having been taken for a boy for a couple of hours?

Justin turned the package, examining all sides and peering at the fine print. "I'd think so. I mean, it's just wadding in different places, isn't it? It's not like there's some specialized plumbing involved, is there?"

"How should I know?"

"Then again, maybe that means they'll leak if we don't have the right kind."

Laura grabbed the package from him and tore it open, withdrawing a diaper with colorful cartoons on it, all in blue. "We'll use these. It has to be better than nothing."

Several minutes later two diapers had been thrown away, but the third one was in place. Sort of.

"Who'd have thought those sticky tapes were so tricky?" Laura grumbled, feeling increasingly frustrated, as they struggled together to dress Pat in green and white overalls. How come the baby business was so complicated? Wasn't Mother Nature supposed to step in and make sure it all came naturally? How were babies expected to survive in this world if people had to wrestle their way through three diapers to keep from taping their hands to their feet, not to mention deciphering instructions that sounded like they'd gone through four translations on their way to English? "Well," she sighed, as the child was finally dressed. "It's bedtime. Which brings us to the next problem: where does she sleep?"

"Guess my bed is the only choice."

"We should have borrowed a crib. My brothers have got at least three between them. Won't she fall off?"

"She's so tiny. We'll put her in the middle, and line something up around her so she can't roll away."

"Are you sure? I could call one of my brothers, and we'd have a crib in half an hour."

"The bed is fine," Justin insisted. He stood up and took the child with him. "There's no need to bring more people into this."

Justin's bedroom was a lot cozier than her own. No upturned crates. No dirty laundry. Just simple furniture in dark wood, and small charcoal drawings decorating the walls. Some dust was the only discernible sin, and a small pile of paperbacks the only objects on the night-stand. The bed was even made.

"My, your mother raised you well," she muttered.

She received a quizzical look in return, as he handed her the child so he'd have his hands free to pull the bedspread off. "What do you mean?"

"Just that everything is so neat. I grew up with two brothers. My mother tried, but they seemed genetically unable to put their socks in the hamper." She put the baby down in the middle of the bed and watched Justin roll up blankets to block Pat's escape routes.

"If nobody had picked up after them, they'd have learned eventually."

"I doubt it."

Justin turned off the lights, leaving only a small lamp. Then they stood, side by side, and watched Pat not go to sleep. Her eyes wide-open, she stared at them with an angry expression, hands curled into small fists, as if daring them to go away.

"Maybe she needs some nighttime ritual," Justin offered. "Maybe we need to read a book to her or something."

"I think she's a little too young to appreciate literature."

"Maybe she's used to someone singing her a lullaby?"

Laura grinned. "A lullaby is an excellent idea, Justin. Go ahead."

"Me?" He looked appalled at the thought. "I don't sing."

She didn't object to his denial, just sent him a knowing grin that had his ears turning slightly pink. "Oh. You hear me in the shower, don't you?"

Laura snickered. "No need to be embarrassed. You've got a great voice."

"Thank you," he mumbled, and turned the conversation quickly back to Pat. "She looks sleepy. Why won't she go to sleep then?"

Pat closed her eyes on a yawn, but forced them open again and didn't look very happy. Her lower lip wobbled as if she were only seconds away from turning the waterworks on.

"She could be scared. She's in unfamiliar surroundings. Maybe if I just lie down with her," Laura said. "If you don't mind?"

"Sure." Justin pulled up a chair next to the bed and sat down, and Laura curled up next to the child, stroking the downy black hair with a finger. The baby relaxed a bit, the angry expression fading to a wary one. "What are we going to do about this, Justin?" she asked drowsily. All of a sudden her eyelids seemed weighted down. She yawned, trying to pry her eyes open.

Mr. Sandman seemed to be targeting the wrong person, Justin thought with amusement, watching Laura struggle to keep her eyes open. "I don't know," he answered, but she didn't hear. Having lost the fight, she was sound asleep, her eyelashes accentuating the dark circles under her eyes.

She looked tired and hungry, Justin thought, staring at her small form, still dressed in her formal working suit, curled around the child. He'd feed both of them tomorrow, he decided. Milk for the little one, grown-up food for the bigger one. Steak. French fries. Ice cream. She needed calories, and lots of them.

Sleepy as she looked, Pat wasn't as quick to fall asleep. Her eyes studied him, reflecting his face as she stared at him with a serious dark blue gaze. He looked away and switched position in the chair as he felt another pang in his heart. That gaze was so familiar.

Babies probably all looked the same, he reasoned. Her eyes hadn't yet taken on their final color. Or his memory was playing tricks on him. It had been many years after all, and he'd only been four years old when Ben was born.

He hadn't been around babies much since then. He hadn't wanted to, had avoided babies whenever he could, but this time, with a small baby abandoned by her parents, he couldn't just stand aside and let her be taken care of by the authorities. He couldn't, especially not when the hue of Pat's eyes was so much like the brightness in little Ben's eyes, those days he'd spent alone with his baby brother, playing with him for hours, trying to change his diaper and keep him fed and clean, and most important to his five-year-old mind, happy and laughing.

He closed his eyes. It had been a long time ago. Ben would be twenty-seven years old now. He didn't often think consciously about Ben, but his little brother was

always there in his heart, would always be a part of who
he was.

He hadn't been able to save Ben. But if he had anything to say about it, this kid wouldn't suffer the same
fate.

"We'll find your folks, kiddo," he whispered, his finger tightly enveloped by Pat's tiny fist. "And if they
aren't up to the job of taking care of you, we'll find you
an adoptive family that is. Promise. You won't grow up
in an orphanage or with someone who mistreats you or
neglects you. I won't let that happen to you."

Pat smiled. She seemed reassured at his words, although logically he knew she didn't understand. She
waved her free arm in the air where it tangled in Laura's
hair, and then promptly fell asleep.

Justin worked his hand free from the baby's grasp. He
pulled a blanket over Laura and tucked a duvet around
the baby.

They made quite a mother-daughter picture, lying
there together, Laura's body protectively huddled around
the infant, and Pat's face turned toward her, nuzzling
into her shoulder.

He grimaced and turned away as he finally labeled the
feeling that was tapping him on the shoulder. A sense
of belonging, togetherness.

He didn't belong, he reminded himself as he quietly
closed the bedroom door and made his bed on the couch.
This was just his next-door neighbor, and an abandoned
child.

They weren't a family. They weren't *his* family.

Laura sat on the floor in Justin's living room, leaning
against the sofa, arms around her knees. She'd at last

managed to get that shower, change into a second pair of French panties, and she'd certainly slept enough last night.

All in all, she was feeling pretty good.

This was not how she'd planned to spend her first Saturday off in ages, but she didn't have a choice. It looked like she'd agreed by omission to Justin's plan of keeping the little one safe until they'd found out more about her parents. She hadn't exactly said yes, but then she hadn't said no either. Instead she'd fallen asleep last night and slept in Justin's bed by Pat's side for almost twelve hours. She'd woken up with two small hands pulling at her hair, and opened her eyes to see an angry face as the little girl fought to reclaim her wayward limbs from the tangle.

She still didn't quite know what she was doing here, in her neighbor's apartment with a child that had been dropped on them out of nowhere. Justin's insistence on not calling the authorities might be justified from his experience, but she couldn't help feeling it was the only correct thing to do. Social Services would know what to do in situations like these, and they'd have people who didn't panic at the thought of changing a diaper.

On the other hand, she'd never been a foster child herself, and didn't know the system first hand. Maybe Justin was right. She didn't know.

Maybe that was the way to go, to neither agree or disagree, and just let the day pass. It was the weekend, anyway. The kid deserved a calm day or two before getting a whole police department on her case. And besides... She looked between Pat and Justin. Yes, she had her suspicions.

Little Pat seemed fine this morning. She was on her

back on the floor, wearing her green overalls, waving her arms and legs around, trying to get a hold of one of the many multicolored toys they'd brought home from the supermarket.

At her side, a large teddy bear with a jaunty green hat watched over her. Justin had done the teddy-shopping. It had taken him forever, too. You couldn't rush those things; the teddy had to be just right, he'd muttered, glaring at her, daring her to laugh, but then his scowl had morphed into a sheepish grin. She'd buried her nose in Pat's shoulder and hidden a smile at this sweet, almost childish, side of him. She smiled again at the memory and glanced up at Justin. He raised an eyebrow in enquiry and she grinned, deciding not to share her thought with him. "It doesn't look like she's missing her mother," she commented instead.

"No." Justin was sitting with a laptop on his knees. He'd been surfing for baby development information for almost an hour now, and before that he'd been checking for any news on missing infants, and come up empty. "If she's not noticing her mother's absence, that could mean she's less than six months old."

"Yeah. But we already knew that from the fact that she isn't sitting by herself yet."

"Yes." He logged off and shut down the laptop. "That's it. I don't think we can narrow it down more. If she's developing normally, she should be somewhere between three and five months."

"Okay." Laura got up off the floor, wincing as her back complained. All those hours at a desk were taking their toll. But it was time to confront Justin about her suspicions. She'd been hoping the thought would occur to him, and he would mention something himself, but no such luck. She took a deep breath. "Justin, we need to talk." ·

"Oh?" His look was wary.

"Yes." She sat down in the sofa opposite him and crossed her legs. Leaning toward him, she took a deep breath in preparation for the question she wanted to ask. Needed to ask. The suspicion was the prime reason she hadn't objected to Justin's demands not to turn the baby over to Social Services—the suspicion that the little girl was already with her father.

"Justin, I know this is a personal question, but it's important: were you..." She looked away as she tried to phrase this the right way. "Were you romantically involved eleven to fifteen months ago?"

"Was I what? Why?"

He wasn't getting it. Better simplify the vocabulary. "Were you sleeping with anyone a year ago?"

Justin stared at her, looking confused and rather offended. "What sort of a question is that?"

Laura sighed. She wasn't handling this all too well. She looked down at the carpet and chose her words carefully. "Justin, our bedroom windows are side by side. If this was your baby, and her mother for some reason wanted to turn her over to you, that could explain this whole thing. Confusing your window with mine would be an easy mistake to make. Could this be your daughter?"

Justin didn't hesitate although the question sent flashes of panic firing through his every nerve. The denial came quickly to his lips. "No. No way. She's not my daughter. That's impossible."

Laura's eyes were sharp and inquisitive, her posture

straight and confident. This was what she must look like in court, he realized, tough and no-nonsense, determined to get to the facts. "Justin, are you sure?" He began to nod, but she kept talking. "She even looks a bit like you. Look, the only way you can be one hundred percent sure is you either didn't sleep with anyone during the period when Pat could have been conceived, or if you know with absolute certainty that none of your partners got pregnant." She stabbed a finger in his direction to emphasize her point. "*Know*, not just assume. So think carefully. Is it possible, even just slightly?"

He gave it a chance and thought back, his heart picking up speed as the possibility for a few moments shimmered real. Then he shook his head slowly. "It's a logical assumption, Laura, but it's not possible. There has to be another explanation."

"Okay."

She didn't look convinced. In fact she looked rather angry, as if certain he was lying to her. "I am a hundred percent sure. I couldn't possibly be the father of this child."

Laura tilted her head and looked at him for a minute. Then her shoulders slumped as he seemed to pass her test. "Okay." She sighed. "It was so logical. Just look at her eyes. And her hair. It's a different shade, but it curls in the back just like yours does when you haven't cut it in a while."

Justin ran his fingers through his hair as he stared at her. It was short enough now, but the knowledge that she'd noticed such details about him was intriguing. "Coincidence, I'm afraid. She's not mine. She can't be."

*   *   *

The weekend passed without any major mishaps, but Sunday evening at dinner, Justin could see that Laura was becoming increasingly antsy.

"I have to go to work tomorrow. I can't possibly take the day off. Why don't they call? Are they expecting us to keep Pat here forever?" She threw her hands out in resignation. "We'll have to call the police, Justin. There is no alternative. Her parents aren't going to come back. They aren't going to call."

Justin plugged the bottle into Pat's mouth, sleeves rolled up and a cloth covering most of his front. They were learning many things the hard way, and he was already a pro at being thrown up on.

"Don't worry. I'll stay home with her tomorrow," he said. "I can probably postpone my appointments. Eat your dessert."

Laura picked up her spoon and started picking at her chocolate chip ice cream. "I shouldn't eat this," she muttered. "Are you trying to turn me into a blimp? There are limits to how much ice cream and chocolate muffins a person should eat in one weekend. Do you eat like this all the time? No, you can't, you wouldn't fit on that flashy motorbike if you did."

Justin tried to look indignant as he grabbed the opening to bring the subject away from his mission of fattening Laura up. "Flashy? My motorcycle is not 'flashy.'"

Laura gave him a "yeah, right" look. "Not flashy, you say?"

"No. It's just cool."

Laura shook her head. "No. Vanity plates, gleaming chrome, washed and waxed at least twice a week.

Flashy.'' She pointed at him with her spoon. "You're a show-off, Justin Bane.''

He grinned. "Well, she is the love of my life. Admit it, you've been dying to try her out.''

"Absolutely not,'' she denied. "I tried a motorbike once, and it's not an experience worth repeating. And it wasn't even a monster like that one, just one of the tiny ones.''

"You mean a moped?''

"Whatever.'' She shrugged. "Had two wheels and attracted more teenage boys than a new issue of *Playboy*. Motorbike, in my book.''

"Philistine,'' Justin muttered. "Pat, remind me to talk motorbikes with you sometime. Girls need to learn to appreciate the cooler things in life.'' He glanced back up at Laura. "So, what did you do to the moped? Did it survive the Laura experience?''

Laura dug into her bowl, and to his satisfaction he could see it was nearly empty. "Well, I sat on it, and my brother told me to turn the…handle, or whatever, to get it going. I did. And the darn thing shot off. On one wheel. With me hanging on to the handlebars, not realizing I was revving the engine, running to keep up with the runaway bike, and screaming at my brother to save me from certain death.''

Justin doubled over Pat, shaking in silent laughter. It earned him an evil look.

"Yes, very funny. It was a while until my brother obliged. He had to pick himself up off the ground first.''

Justin snickered. "You should have screamed at your brother to save the *bike* from certain death. That would have gotten his attention.''

Laura groaned. "You're right. That bike even had a

name. And he's still talking about the supposed 'injury' I did to that thing. I don't think he's ever forgiven me.''

''A man's motorcycle isn't a 'thing,' Laura. See? This is one of the biggest gulfs between men and women. Women just don't understand.'' He shook his head, hiding a grin at seeing her increased frustration. ''What I don't understand is why the relationship experts never discuss this issue. Women would be so much easier to deal with if they understood things like football and machines.''

''*Women* need to be easier to deal with? We're not the ones who…'' Laura slapped his arm as he finally failed to hide his grin. ''You're trying to bait me, aren't you?''

Justin snickered, rocking Pat who was no longer interested in her milk. ''I thought you'd be used to that, with that brother of yours.''

''Yeah. My brother is a mechanic now. I take my car to him every now and then. He fixes it for free, but in return I have to suffer through him telling his co-workers an embellished version of that moped story every single time. He thinks this is a fair exchange. I'm in doubt, myself.''

''Aw, poor Laura.''

Laura pushed the empty ice cream bowl away and glared at him. ''You'd look more sincere if you weren't grinning. How about you, got any evil brothers? Or sisters to torture?''

''No.'' The question still hurt. Quarter of a century later, and it was still painful to remember Ben. ''I had a brother once, but he died a long time ago. He was just a baby.''

''Oh. I'm so sorry.''

There was sympathy in her eyes that he didn't want. He shrugged. "It was a long time ago." He pushed his own bowl of ice cream, untouched and slightly melting, until it was right under her nose, and distracted her with a question just as she opened her mouth to protest. "Didn't you say you had more than one brother?"

"Yeah. Two of them. The three of you should get along great. He's also a macho chauvinist with a football and cars obsession. Runs a sporting goods store."

"What kind of stories does he tell about his sister?"

Laura shuddered and absently began to dig into his ice cream. "Well, there are the animals. The bugs, the frogs, the snakes. He tells the story of how he was supposed to baby-sit me for an afternoon when I was four, and kept me in my room the entire time by the simple method of placing a shoebox with spiders in it outside my door."

"You must have had a fascinating childhood."

"I'm getting my revenge. Both of them have two boys of their own now." Laura cackled.

"I bet they get lots of noisy toys from Aunt Laura."

"How did you guess? I even got Gavin his own drum set last Christmas. He'll love me forever."

"What if the little monsters get a baby sister? Do you have a protection plan?"

"Of course. I'll threaten acute cool-presents withdrawal if they don't treat her like a lady." She stared down into the bowl. "Hey? I finished all the ice cream. Yours too."

Justin smiled. "Good. Can't have you sticking poor Pat with those ribs." He passed the child over. She'd fallen asleep, leaving the last inch of milk in the bottle. Frowning, Laura smoothed the T-shirt over her middle, as if to check that her ribs wouldn't puncture the baby. "Being 'scrawny' is fashionable, in case you hadn't noticed," she said defensively.

On an impulse, Justin leaned over and touched her mouth with his, then stood up and started loading the dishwasher. "Ice cream," he explained at her startled expression. "You had some on your lip."

He'd kissed her. It was a kiss much like the ones he gave Pat, and just one step up from scrubbing her face with a washcloth, but her hormones didn't seem to mind those little details. The very stereotype of a silly female, she was letting one innocent kiss turn her emotions upside down.

She pushed the sleeping baby into Justin's arms and both of them out of the room with instructions for a fresh diaper and bed. She loaded the dishwasher and tried to stop thinking about his novel way of cleaning up ice cream. It had just been a silly gesture.

After all, she was scrawny. Not his type, any more than he was hers. Despite the chocolate eyes.

She finished cleaning up the kitchen in record time and went off to search for Justin. He'd distracted her from the discussion on what to do about baby Pat, but it was a discussion they couldn't postpone much longer.

She found them in the bathroom, Justin kneeling by the side of the tub, floating the baby in a few inches of water. His shoulders were tense and his brow knotted in concentration. The little one was a squirming eel in the water. Justin was already soaked, from the top of his head down to his middle.

As views went, that one was worth the admittance fee.

"How's it going?"

Justin looked up, his face and hair wet. "You're just in time. Can you hold out the towel so I can put her directly on it?"

Laura got the towel ready, and Justin lifted the baby out of the water and wrapped the towel around her quickly. "See?" he said triumphantly. "If we wrap her in a towel the same moment we pick her up, she doesn't cry because she doesn't get cold. I think I'm getting the hang of this."

"Yeah. You'll make a great father someday."

The glance he sent her was as incredulous as if she'd suggested he give his motorcycle up for adoption, and incongruent with the way he was cuddling the baby to his chest. "No, I won't. Could you find something for her to sleep in?"

When Pat was asleep, Laura cornered Justin off. "Okay, so you're staying home with the baby tomorrow. What about the day after? We can't keep this up. We'll get in trouble."

"We give it a couple of days," he said stubbornly. "Her parents left her in our care. A couple of days, and then we'll contact the authorities. We can't shirk our responsibilities to this child."

The obstinate line of his jaw told her that this compromise was the best he would do. Laura sighed, and considered the alternatives. She snapped her fingers as one occurred to her. "What about hiring a private investigator? If the mother won't come to us, perhaps we could track her down, and get an explanation."

"What will he investigate, Laura? There isn't exactly an overabundance of clues."

She shrugged. "They're the experts. Who knows what is a clue? The clothing labels, perhaps. And there might still be some fingerprints left on the window pane. Justin, let's call a PI. That little girl needs her family.''

Justin was silent for a moment, then shrugged. ''Okay, if nothing happens tomorrow, we'll hire an investigator.''

CHAPTER FOUR

PAT wasn't a fan of the nighttime.

As soundly as she slept for hours on end during the day, she wouldn't sleep more than an hour or two at a time during the night. It hadn't been so hard before, when both of them had been there to take turns, but now Laura had work in the morning so he had insisted she get some sleep.

It wasn't as easy to do this on his own. Not as much fun, either. Laura had the greatest sense of humor at three in the morning. Her sarcasm tended to scorch holes in his flesh, but it was worth it.

At four in the morning, he gave up on trying to get Pat to sleep. The warm weather didn't help—both of them were hot and sweaty, and the little lady seemed determined not to fall asleep.

"We'll go for a walk, Pat," he told her. "I'll show you the swings in the backyard. How about that? Maybe we'll try them out and see if the rocking helps you sleep."

The autumn night still felt more like summer, and he made do with a pair of jeans, but he didn't dare take any risks with Pat. He wrapped her in a few layers of the warmest of the green garments in her tote bag, and headed for the front door.

Pat stopped crying as they stepped out into the dark night. He shuffled down the stairs carefully, always terrified he'd miss a step and drop the baby, and wandered around the house to the backyard.

"You know, my brother Ben was also a fussy sleeper," he told Pat as he sat down on the tire swing. "He kept waking up, and I never knew what he wanted or what was wrong with him." He adjusted the child in his arms. "He was really heavy. It was hard for me to carry him around because I wasn't very big myself. Maybe that was what he wanted, just to be held and carried around a bit. Just like you do."

He pushed at the ground to set the swing in motion, holding the memory of his brother in his mind. He hadn't been able to carry Ben around much. Instead he'd sat on the floor with him, stroked his head and rocked him back and forth. Sometimes it had worked, and Ben had settled down, smiling and gurgling. And sometimes it hadn't, and Ben had screamed louder and louder, his face red and his little body trembling, and there'd been nothing Justin could do.

He clenched his jaw, thinking of the day when they'd been taken away from their father. He'd been relieved at first, because Ben had been so unhappy, crying all the time, coughing and screaming. The first night away from home they'd slept together in a tiny room, Justin's cot on the floor next to Ben's crib. Ben had whimpered most of the night, but usually settled down when Justin grabbed his hand.

Then the next day Ben had been taken away to see the doctor. He'd never come back.

He took a deep breath of the fresh night air, and held Pat closer. The rocking motions of the swing had worked. She was burrowing her head into his chest, fast asleep. "I did try to find him, you understand," he whispered. "I really did. For months I threw a nonstop tantrum, and then I ran away a few times, stupid enough to think I might find him. It never did any good. They never told me what happened to him. It wasn't until years and years later that I found out that he'd died soon after. He was already sick when they took us away."

He stayed there, holding Pat in his arms and Ben in his thoughts, rocking back and forth until the swing lost its momentum and finally wasn't moving at all.

"Well," he murmured, forcing himself to move back to the present. "Shall we see if you wake up the minute I put you to bed? I wouldn't mind a small nap myself."

He was at his door before he realized the slight hitch in that plan. He sagged against the door, cursing. "Damn it!"

As soon as the knock reached her through confused dreams, Laura felt guilty, even before she woke up. She sat up in bed, for a moment disoriented, but panic nevertheless swamping her, and then bolted out from under the cover, shooting toward the door. Something must have happened to Pat.

She shouldn't have left Justin alone with the baby. But he'd insisted that he'd be alone with her all day long, so he might as well take the night shift, too, so she could get some sleep and prepare for the week at work. Besides, as he'd pointed out, despite the supposed chromosomal advantages, she wasn't any better at this than he was.

And now it was almost five in the morning, and something was wrong. Why else would Justin be knocking at her door at this hour?

"What's wrong?" she asked as soon as she'd yanked

the door open, looking him and the baby over. "I heard her cry earlier, but there hasn't been any sound for a while." She leaned closer for a better look at Pat. No blood. Fast asleep. So far, so good.

Justin smiled sheepishly. "Nothing's wrong. I'm just locked out."

"You're locked out?" she repeated, relief making her slightly dizzy. There was nothing wrong with Pat. "With the baby? How'd you do that?"

Justin shrugged with one shoulder, the one baby Pat wasn't sleeping on. "We were hot, and she wouldn't sleep. So I decided we'd walk around in the backyard a bit."

"And you forgot your keys?"

"Yeah."

Laura threw the door open for him to enter and stepped back, grateful that guilt had made her spend those few free hours last night cleaning up. The place no longer looked as if it had been burglarized.

Men look so sexy with a baby on their shoulder, she thought, staring at the two of them. Especially in the middle of the night, smelling faintly of a mixture of baby vomit and baby powder, barefoot and bare-chested with their hair mussed up and eyes sleepy.

Well, at least this one did.

Rethinking the whole issue of Eau de Baby Vomit, Laura came to the conclusion that it was also a distinct possibility she was just nuts.

"Want to call a locksmith?" she asked, struggling to get her thoughts under control.

"Nah. My bedroom window is open. I'll just climb out yours and in mine."

Why did that sound suggestive?

Yes, she sighed, as she lead the way to her bedroom, she *was* nuts.

"I'm sorry for waking you up," Justin said, still keeping his voice low for Pat's sake. "Can I put her in your bed while I get my keys?"

"Sure. And no problem. I should be getting up soon anyway. My brother was going to come by to take a look at my car before I left for work, so I set my alarm extra early."

Justin carefully tucked Pat between two pillows and started climbing out the window. He sent her a dark look from the fire escape. "Your working hours are ridiculous."

"I'm new at the company. I need to impress."

His answer was an unconvinced grunt, and then he vanished.

Laura crawled into bed with the little girl, snuggling up to the tiny body. Very carefully, she removed some of the outer layers of clothes. The baby was sweating. "Will the two of you be okay today?" she whispered. "I feel terrible about leaving you behind, but to tell you the truth, Justin is probably better than I am in this baby business. I'm terrified I'll break your arm every time I put you in a new shirt."

Pat's eyes opened, and she smiled.

"Oops. I woke you up. Sorry." Laura let the little girl grab a hold of her thumb. "I really should have called my brothers and sisters-in-law. They're got tons of baby experience. They'd know what to do with you."

"We're doing fine," Justin said as he swung his feet inside the window and jumped in. "Bringing more people into this will just cause trouble. If we're lucky, it'll all be solved today."

"Do you have some problem with using doors?"

He shrugged. "It was quicker this way."

"Of course," she muttered. "Daredevil motorcyclists. Speed is everything."

Justin grinned. He sat down on the other side of Pat and made faces at the little girl, who gave him one of her irresistible smiles in return. "Laura, have you decided what to do, if we find out that her parents really expect you to take care of her permanently?"

"That's not going to happen."

"But if it does." His face was serious, but he didn't look at her. Instead he kept his gaze fixed on Pat. "What will you do?"

Sure as she was that this was a scenario she'd never have to face, something in her stomach grew sharp edges and started bouncing around. "That's impossible. I can't look after a baby."

"Weren't you planning on ever having any?"

"Yes. I mean no. I mean, I wasn't planning. If I ever meet the right man, I guess. If I ever have the time for a family. I don't know. I certainly didn't plan on becoming a single mother for an orphaned doorstep baby."

"Do you want a family?"

"Yes. I grew up in a really close family. Horrid though my brothers were, I still love them. What about you?"

"I'm not in touch with my relatives."

"Do you want a family of your own?"

Justin leaned over Pat, shutting Laura out. "It's not something that's in the picture."

"Families don't fit your lifestyle?"

"Something like that." He stood and lifted Pat with him. "Have a good day at work."

Laura jumped to her feet and searched the jumbled mess on her nightstand for pen and paper. "Here. My number at work. If anything comes up, call me."

Justin grabbed the piece of paper and jammed it in his pocket. "Sure."

The doorbell sounded, causing Pat to whimper and wave her arms in sudden panic.

"It's open!" a voice called. "Sis, you really shouldn't leave your door open like this."

"Dammit!" Laura whispered, looking Justin and the baby over. Steve was early. She really didn't need the aggravation. Would Justin and Pat fit in her small closet? Under the bed? Behind the curtains?

"I'm afraid I forgot my invisibility cloak," Justin whispered with a grin, and Laura shook her head in irritation.

"I hate it when you do that," she muttered.

"Do what?" he asked innocently, and she glared at him.

"Read my mind and then laugh at me."

Justin chuckled. "Well, you were looking at me like I was a particularly nasty-smelling piece of garbage that needed to be ejected out the nearest airlock. What's the problem, overprotective brother come to defend sister's virtue? Will I need my boxing gloves?"

Her brother's footsteps were approaching. "Sis? Fall asleep again?" Laura shot toward the door, belatedly realizing that all she had to do was talk to her brother outside of the bedroom, and there wouldn't be any questions, or embellished tales of a man and a baby in her bedroom early in the morning.

Steve, overprotective? Nope. Overenthusiastic matchmaker? Yep. She'd have to keep the two of them from meeting, or Justin would be roped into Sunday dinner at her mother's house before he could even open his mouth to tell them families didn't fit his lifestyle.

"Oof!" Steve recoiled as she ran into him, his hands grabbing her shoulders. "Where's the fire? And why are you still in your robe? Sleeping in? Weren't we going to fix your car this morning before you left for work?"

There were several disadvantages to being short. One was that it was impossible to hide anything behind you. People could just look over your head, and Steve, brown eyes now wide open and interested, was staring at something inside the room. She guessed it wasn't her unmade bed or the mess on her nightstand that drew his attention. Nope. It would be the six feet of half-naked male sitting on her bed. Laura stepped back, resigned, and shrugged. "Morning, Steve."

Justin nodded to her brother. "Hi. I'm Justin Bane. From next door."

Steve's eyes narrowed and he pointed at Justin, his finger waggling as his brow creased in thought. "I've heard about you, I think. Wait, you're the motorcycle guy, right? Laura's told me all about you."

Oh, Lord.

She hadn't mentioned him *that* much, Laura thought grouchily, her thoughts toward her brother less than hospitable. She'd only mentioned Justin because he shared the motorcycle passion with her brothers, who'd admired his bike every time they came over. How did Steve remember? And why did he have to make it sound like she'd been prattling about him to her family like a teenager with a crush?

Steve's grin now reached halfway around his head and only widened when she glared at him. Oh. That was it.

The matchmaking schemes. He was doing this on purpose. "I'm Steve," he said to Justin. "Biggest brother and fierce protector. Fixer of cars and mender of washing machine. And of course, I'm her favorite."

Justin stood up, taking Pat with him, and shook Steve's hand. Steve's eyes widened even more at the sight of the baby in Justin's arms. He poked his sister after taking a moment to recover. "What a cozy domestic scene. You didn't tell me you were a stepmom. How long has this been going on?"

"I'm not a stepmom. Nothing's going on. The baby was—"

Justin broke in. "I was alone with the baby, and needed some help. Your sister's been very helpful."

"He's not the baby's..."

The last word was bitten off by the sudden presence of Justin's mouth pressed against hers just long enough to stop her talking. The pinch at her upper arm also helped. "Thank you so much for your help with my daughter, Laura. See you tonight." He stepped back, leaving Laura speechless, and nodded again to Steve. "Nice to meet you." He walked toward the door, then turned around. "By the way, are you the one who terrorized her with spiders, or the one whose moped she nearly ruined?"

Steve blew out air in a long-suffering sigh. "My moped. My Suzy. Three huge scratches and a dent. Your bike is a beauty, by the way."

"I limped for days, and after more than a decade you're still talking about a few invisible scratches!"

The men sent each other looks of mutual understanding, and Laura realized this was a lost cause. Justin wasn't even noticing the way she was rubbing her arm where he'd pinched her to make sure she didn't tell her brother their circumstances.

She leaned over the baby in Justin's arms and planted a soft kiss on her forehead. "Be good, Pat," she whispered, trying to ignore the warm magnetism of the man holding the child. "See you tonight."

Justin was smiling when she straightened up again. "We'll be fine." He took Pat's hand between his thumb and forefinger and helped her wave goodbye. Laura looked after him as he walked out of the apartment, softly talking to the baby.

For a man who claimed babies didn't fit his lifestyle, he sure was doing a good job.

Steve put his arm around her shoulder and squeezed. "Well, sis, are you going to get dressed and come watch me fix your car, and tell me all about your new boyfriend and his kid?"

She put her hands on his chest and pushed him backward out of her bedroom, closing the door in his face. His laughter drifted through the door. "You can hide, but you can't run!" he called. "I'm honor-bound to take all stories of your romantic involvements back to Mom. You know that. Especially if they involve stepgrandchildren. Gives her a chance to do her 'that child needs a brother or a sister' routine."

Irritation spurring her on, Laura got ready for work in record time, glad to have taken the time to do a few loads of laundry between the diapers and baby feedings.

Today she was *not* wearing French poetry.

She found Steve flung on her sofa, aimlessly flipping between channels on her television. She walked in front of the television and crossed her arms.

"Justin is not my boyfriend," she informed Steve.

"And I don't appreciate it when you try to embarrass me in front of my friends."

"Sorry." Steve grinned to show how sorry he was. "Force of habit. In my defense, he didn't kiss you like he was just a friend."

"Well, he is," she retorted. Having set the record straight, she turned to the front door. She was amused to notice a thin layer of dust on her briefcase, where it sat against the wall by the front door. It had been a while since anything work-related had gathered dust.

"By the way, that's not Justin's kid," she added when they were at the bottom of the stairs and she could be reasonably sure that Justin wouldn't appear to kiss her mouth shut.

Steve fetched his toolkit from his SUV and opened the hood of her car. "She's not? Oh. I thought he said it was his daughter."

"Yeah. He did. He's worried you'll call the cops on us."

"Ouch!" Steve rubbed the top of his head where it had hit the open hood. "Run that by me again. Call the cops? What are you talking about? Did he kidnap the kid or something?"

Laura told him the story, pausing pointedly every time the absurdity of the situation made him stop his work on her car. If he was going to get the whole story, he might as well work for it.

As a result, he was pronouncing her car reasonably healthy around the same time as she was wrapping up her complaints about how Justin had refused to go to the police.

"Well, sounds logical to me," Steve had the gall to say. He stared down into the engine with a frown, and ran a hand through his hair, leaving black streaks in the dark blond mane. Not an uncommon sight. "What else is there to do but wait for the parents to be in touch?"

Laura raised her gaze heavenward. "You're just saying that because he sympathized with you over the scratches on your bike."

Steve was again bent over the engine, his words distorted as they floated up to her. "No, really, I mean, if someone asked you to look after their child, you look after the child. You don't dump her on the authorities if you're at all able to take care of her yourself." He straightened up, and closed the hood. "You should be fine for now. But it's not a long-term fix. Next weekend I'll take it to the shop for a closer look."

"Thanks, Steve. I'd kiss you, but you're too filthy." She sent him a finger kiss. "There. That'll have to do."

Steve grinned and made a valiant effort to rub most of the dirt off his hands with something that had probably been a towel in a previous life. After only succeeding in smearing his hands even more, he gave up and instead lunged toward Laura with a growl, his black palms aiming for her cheeks. She shrieked and backed away, stumbling until he grabbed her wrist to keep her from falling over.

"Sorry, sis," he said, somewhat contrite. "I was just teasing. Wasn't going to touch you. Didn't mean to make you fall."

Laura sighed the long-suffering sigh of the little sister, looking at her filthy wrist. She pushed the sleeve gingerly up her arm, hoping she wouldn't have to change clothes. Or figure out a way to get motor oil out of silk. "I'm not twelve anymore, Steve. It's no longer your brotherly duty to torture me to show me that you love me.''

"So the two of you have been playing house all weekend?''

Laura glanced up toward Justin's window. "Sort of.''

"You like him, don't you?''

"What if I do? Are you going to write *Laura loves Justin* on the school wall? You're as bad as Mom.''

"We just want you happy.''

"I am happy.''

"You work too much.''

She'd heard that recently. Laura reclaimed her car keys and opened her door. "I'm establishing a career. I want financial security. You of all people should understand why.''

"We didn't have much money, that's true, but Mom and Dad were happy together. We were a happy family, weren't we? Money can't buy happiness.''

How that cliché got on her nerves, Laura thought with a big sigh. "It goes a long way toward the down payment,'' she retorted, and waved her brother goodbye.

Laura's right hand grabbed the phone for the seventh time that afternoon, and for the seventh time, her left hand intervened and firmly returned the phone to its cradle.

They were doing fine, she chastised herself. Justin had her number in case anything came up. Why did she think she was indispensable to the little girl's life? She was just as much a novice as Justin was in the baby business.

But keeping her mind on work wasn't easy. She glanced at the clock and sighed. If she worked anywhere close to normal hours, she should be going home now, and she could hear the offices empty of people, and the footsteps mostly going in the same direction—toward the elevators and freedom.

She pinched the bridge of her nose and forced herself to look back down at the document she was reading. It was a new case, a case she'd been assigned, and a case she hated.

It wasn't her place to pass moral judgment on her clients, but this mother seemed determined to get custody of her son as a revenge against the father, who'd had sole custody for three years now. Laura hated this case, hated having to represent a side she didn't believe in, but at this stage in her career she didn't have much choice. She just did her best with what was handed to her.

Two more hours, and then she'd go home. Home to Justin and Pat, and all that needed to be done. Bathe and feed. Wash green baby clothes. Sing lullabies. Call the private investigator.

Call the PI. Laura shot to her feet. They'd planned to call an investigator today. She better get home, or they'd never reach anyone before closing time.

With a secret mixture of relief and anticipation, Laura did the unthinkable for the second time in the last few days—left the building while it was still daylight.

At home, she went directly to Justin's apartment, and he answered the door with a grumpy-looking baby on his arms.

"Hi…" She held out her arms to take Pat, astonished to realize how much she'd missed the child. And Justin, too. She shook the feeling off, irritated at how her emotions were betraying her. She couldn't get attached to their illusion of a family. It wouldn't last. "What's wrong?"

"I don't think anything's wrong," Justin answered as he deposited the baby in her arms. "She's just been grouchy and sulking. Maybe she missed you."

Sure enough, a wide smile appeared on Pat's face as she squirmed to get closer to Laura, tiny hands tangling in her hair and pulling, a string of nonsensical vowels dancing from her mouth.

She cleared her throat of an annoying lump and followed Justin inside. "You'll be pleased to know that my brother agrees with you."

"Steve? About what?"

"About keeping the baby for a few days to see if the parents turn up."

"You told him?" Justin's face darkened. "How could you tell him? You knew I didn't want you to tell him!"

He didn't exactly believe in family loyalties, did he? "He's my brother, Justin. We're family. He can be trusted." She sat down and gave him a reproving look. "Besides, if we're doing the right thing, we've got nothing to hide, do we?"

"It's safest if nobody knows about this until it's all over and we've found her mother."

"You don't have any close family, do you?"

"What's that got to do with anything? Aren't you home early?" he added.

"Yes. I remembered we have to call the PI."

"I already did. He's coming over around six."

"Nobody called today, did they?"

"You mean her folks? Nope. Not a word."

Laura sighed. "Great. Well, I'll go home for a shower and change clothes, then. Be right back."

"Sure. We'll take a nap in the meantime. She's been refusing to sleep all afternoon. Wait a moment." He fished in his pocket for something. "I got you a key."

"A key?"

"To the apartment."

"A key to your apartment?" she parroted, as he put the key in her palm and curled her fingers around it when she didn't do so herself. Somehow, this felt bizarre. She'd never been given the key to a man's apartment before.

"What's the big deal?"

"Nothing. Just that I'm not used to having keys to other people's apartments."

Justin grinned. "Well, I'm not used to giving them out, so that makes us even."

"Right. Thanks. Okay, I'll be back in a little while." She kissed Pat and left for next door, fastening Justin's key on her key chain before opening her own door.

There was a pile of mail in her mailbox, the usual monthly bills. She grabbed the whole bunch and quickly scanned them, throwing one by one on top of her dresser for later attention. There was never anything interesting in the mail. This time wasn't any different. Just bills and junk mail.

And a white piece of paper, folded in two.

CHAPTER FIVE

THE mystery of Pat's paternity was solved.

Hiring a PI seemed to have done the trick. He wasn't even here yet, but already there had been results.

Laura sat at her kitchen table, wearing green rubber gloves and holding the letter with salad tongs. There didn't seem to be much need to preserve fingerprints, but to be on the safe side she wasn't taking any chances of ruining the evidence.

The letter explained a thing or two. Justin would also have some explaining to do about the stated impossibility of him having fathered that lovely baby girl.

A lovely baby girl named Jenna.

Why had he denied the very possibility?

And why did she feel so betrayed by his denial?

She rested her chin on her knuckles and stared out the kitchen window into the colorful crown of the maple tree outside. She'd trusted him—that was the problem. She'd believed him, believed that he wasn't the type to abandon pregnant girlfriends, to deny the responsibility of fatherhood when it was thrust upon him. She'd been wrong.

But at least she was off the hook now. For better or worse, the baby was with her father. All she had to do was show him the letter.

She stood up and went back to Justin's apartment, letting herself in with the key. The living room was empty, and she headed straight for his bedroom where she expected the baby to be napping. She entered without knocking. After having spent a significant portion of the weekend sharing that bedroom with him and his child, she felt she had the right to. Hell, she had the right to throw a bucket of ice water over his head if she wanted to. He deserved it.

Justin was napping beside his daughter.

He was sleeping on his stomach, his face turned toward Jenna, who was just as sound asleep, anchored by rolls of blankets on three sides and chairs lined up by the side of the bed. Much to Laura's annoyance, they looked adorable together.

"Justin?" she whispered, only for the child's sake. Otherwise she would have woken him with a yell. He deserved it. He'd made a woman pregnant, and then denied it was even possible. Men! How could they be so irresponsible? So cruel?

Justin didn't respond. How could he have fallen so fast asleep in the twenty minutes since she'd left? He must have stayed up with the baby all night.

He didn't even move, except to tuck his hands under his pillow and snuggle deeper into the bed. Not so different from Pat...from Jenna. The eyes were the same, the black shadow of long lashes identical. Her gaze rested on him far too long before she looked up at the ceiling and sighed at herself.

Even now, when she was feeling hurt and betrayed, she felt like crawling in there and snuggling up against him. What was wrong with her?

Time to wake up Mr. Dad and give him a piece of her mind.

"Justin!" she repeated, a bit louder. "Get up."

"Um?" Finding no solace in burying his face in the

pillow, Justin lifted his head for a disoriented second, then slumped back down, this time burrowing his head under the pillow.

Well, tough.

"Wake up," she said as sharply as she dared, wishing she had the guts—and the strength—to push him off the side of the bed. "Get up, Justin, we need to talk. The mystery is solved. I've found the baby's father."

"You have? That's great. Who? How?" He struggled up on his elbow and pushed his hair out of his eyes, squinting at her. She took a deep breath and found herself needing to look at the ceiling again.

"Let's talk in the living room so we don't disturb Jenna."

"Jenna?" He looked over at the child, sleeping with a thumb in her mouth. "That's her name? I was really getting used to Pat."

Laura turned around and waited for him in the living room. He followed a few moments later, yawning. "Okay. Where's her father? Is he fit to take care of her? Does he even want her?"

"I'm not sure," she said icily, crossing her arms on her chest. "I would guess that he doesn't want her."

Justin's face froze. "He doesn't? The bastard." He glanced toward the bedroom and lowered his voice. "Poor kid."

How deep could denial go? "Justin…" Laura shook her head. "You don't understand. There was a letter in my mailbox. My guess was right. Despite all your protests, it turns out this is your daughter."

Justin didn't even flinch, just raised his eyebrow in confused surprise. "No, she's not."

"She is," Laura insisted. How could he still protest?

The kid looked like him, had been left—almost—in his apartment, and now there was a letter identifying him as the father. And he still denied it? "She was left in my apartment by accident, her mother obviously thought this was your place."

Justin looked fully awake now. Awake and furious. "Laura, I told you. She is not mine. It's a mistake. If she were mine, I'd take responsibility, there's no question about that."

She shoved the note under his nose, only then realizing by his strange look that she was still wearing the green gloves and holding the letter with the salad tongs. "See. The note has your name, delivered at this address. How can that be a mistake?"

Justin grabbed the note from her, salad tongs and all, and read the note, his eyes widening. Then he read it again, his lips moving as he whispered the words slowly as if to understand them better.

"Justin. You have now met your daughter, Jenna, born on June 3. I can't take care of her, so you must. Good luck. For your sake, I hope your new bimbo has mother instincts," he finished, brow creasing. "Signed, Linda." He shook his head and turned an angry glance at her. "What the hell is this?"

She smirked. She'd noticed that part of the note. "Does your new bimbo have mother instincts?"

"Well, you tell me."

"What do you mean?"

Justin dropped the note to the table and started pacing the floor. "Obviously, not only is this a case of mistaken identity, but the mother thinks we're living together. You're the one she saw enter the apartment. She probably waited out on the fire escape, remember? She assumed this was the father's apartment and that you were his wife or girlfriend.''

"I'm the bimbo?"

Justin nodded.

"I'm not a bimbo!"

He gestured toward the note. "Yell at Linda, not me."

"Well, who is Linda?"

"I have no idea. I don't know a Linda."

"Well, obviously she knows you! Intimately!"

Justin's dark eyes were serious as he stopped right in front of her. He lifted her chin and stared into her eyes. "Laura, would you please, just for a minute, acknowledge the possibility that I may actually be telling you the truth?"

Laura pulled herself away from him and sat down at the kitchen table, rubbing her temples. "The circumstantial evidence is substantial, Justin, which makes it hard to believe you. Maybe you should recheck your dating schedule. It says here that Jenna was born in June. So she was conceived in September. Any bells chiming yet?"

Justin shook his head. "She's not mine."

"I suppose that your lovers are all disposable and quickly forgotten, but you really should remember the ones you risk creating new human beings with."

Justin's gaze turned from cold to icy. "Why am I under attack from you?"

"You're denying being that baby's father despite overwhelming evidence. I don't like men who shirk their parental duties."

Justin swore. "Fine. You're choosing not to believe me. Why? What have I done that makes me so untrustworthy in your eyes?"

"I don't know you very well, do I?" she shot back.

"We've practically been living together for a whole weekend. I thought we were getting to know each other pretty well. I am not this child's father, Laura. Someone else is."

"Someone else named Justin who lives in this house?"

"I have no idea why she's here, or why the note is addressed to me." He glared at her. "Let's not forget that she was left in your apartment, not mine. Are you sure you don't happen to have an ex boyfriend named Justin?"

She ignored the absurd question. "Will you take a DNA test, to make sure?"

"That's the only way you'll believe me, isn't it?"

He seemed pretty sure, Laura acknowledged. Sure, and hurt over her refusal to believe him. Maybe he was the type who didn't believe contraceptives ever failed. Maybe he'd had a vasectomy that hadn't worked. She opened her mouth, but just managed to stop herself from interrogating him about that part. No matter what their circumstances, it was none of her business. She shrugged. "You've been named as the father, so the next logical step is to test it. The DNA test will prove it, one way or another. It doesn't matter what I believe."

"It matters to me that you believe me, Laura."

"Why?"

Justin sat down next to her and touched her cheek for a moment, the back of his hand cool against her heated skin. "Do you really have to ask?"

No. She didn't. Something had been happening here, in between taking care of Jenna and doing ordinary things—family things. Something special. It wasn't something she'd been looking for, not even something she was sure she wanted…but for a while it had been something special. She shook her head, avoiding Justin's question and its meaning.

Justin looked back down at the sheet of paper identifying him as Jenna's father. Something seemed to occur to him and he looked up at her again. "This is addressed to me. You opened my mail?"

Laura flushed. "Of course not! Linda thinks you're living in my apartment, remember? This was in my mailbox, and it wasn't in an envelope. It was just a folded page. I just looked to see what it was, and the entire text jumped at me. I don't snoop."

"Fine. I'll return the favor and give you the benefit of the doubt."

"Wait, let me get a bucket, your sarcasm is dripping."

His face suddenly creased in laughter, disarming her completely. Then the frown reappeared as quickly as it had disappeared. He stood up, paced the floor for a moment, then fell down into the sofa and stared out the window. "What a mess. I can't believe all this is happening to the poor child."

Could she believe him? Could this all be a mistake? Or was he just in denial, refusing to acknowledge the fact that he might be a father?

"We know her name now," she said. "If we go to the police, that might make it easier to track her folks down."

"No police yet."

"Justin!"

"You think she's mine, don't you? Well, as her accused father, I decide that we keep her here until we've seen what the PI has to say."

"But you've been saying she isn't yours!"

"You think she's mine, and I'm keeping her until I prove otherwise."

Laura slapped the table with her palm. "And they say women are illogical?"

Justin shrugged. "The detective will be here soon. There should be fingerprints on the letter, or on my window. We have to get to the bottom of this. The mother will be able to tell us if she had aliens abduct me and impregnate her. You'd believe that, wouldn't you?"

Laura pointed to the letter. "You realize that this means that the mother isn't coming back for her baby, Justin. She assumes Pat—I mean, Jenna, is with her father. That means we either have to find her family, or deliver her to the authorities."

Justin's face had again taken on the stubborn look she'd come to recognize far too well, but the argument was postponed when the doorbell rang.

It was the private detective, Mr. Harris, burly and dark, looking rather grouchy as he peered around the apartment. Justin told him the whole story, how Laura had come home to find the baby girl in her bed, and showed him the note.

Mr. Harris read the note, and his eyebrows shot up. "So this is your daughter?"

Justin shrugged. "So the note says," he answered.

"And you want me to find the mother? This Linda?"

"Yes."

He pulled a notebook out of his pocket and wielded a pen. "Okay. What's her last name, and last known address?"

"I have no idea."

Mr. Harris's left eyebrow shot toward his receding hairline again. "You don't know her last name?"

"No."

"Well. Okay." He wielded the pen again. "A brief physical description then? Height, weight, hair color, that type of thing."

"I have no idea."

The hand holding the pen sagged. "You don't remember what this woman looks like?"

"Nope."

"How about her age?" Mr. Harris asked, hopelessly. "In her twenties, thirties, forties?"

"I don't know anything about her. All we know is what it says on the note."

Mr. Harris didn't hide his feelings very well, and oozed cold against Justin for the rest of his visit. He looked over Jenna's clothes, and the bag they had come in, put the letter in a plastic bag and tucked it in his briefcase; and dusted the window in Laura's bedroom, revealing a plethora of fingerprints that had Laura squirming in embarrassment. It didn't take a private investigator to see that the window hadn't been cleaned in months. Not since she'd moved in.

"I've got a buddy in the police department, so we should find out soon enough if there is a match on the fingerprints," he said at last. "I'll get back to you tomorrow." He paused, looking Justin up and down. "In the meantime, it would be a good idea for you to get a DNA test, or a blood test at the very least. So that you can prove that you're the father, just in case."

Justin held back his frustration. He hadn't corrected the man's assumption that the letter was right, that he was the baby's father, and he'd stopped Laura from mentioning anything. He didn't care what Harris thought. Anything to avoid losing Jenna to the authorities.

Laura's face was red with anger as she closed the door after the PI. "I was trying to be polite, since he's supposed to be good at his job, but what business has he being rude to you?" she burst out. "What is he, the Morals Police? He has no idea what the circumstances are, but jumps to the conclusion that you're some random womanizer who picks up ten women a week and can't even remember them."

"*He's* jumping to conclusions?" Justin asked mildly, and watched Laura begin another tirade, but stop before she'd done much more than open her mouth. She looked so confused that he had to smile. "It's okay, Laura. I know everything points to me. I don't like it that you don't trust my words, but I know it's difficult to believe that I'm not her father. And don't worry about my feelings. I really couldn't care less what that man thinks."

The contrite look on her face told him that she understood the implicit meaning: that he did care what *she* thought. "I'm sorry, Justin." She looked down, biting her lip. "I want to believe you. I do believe now that you think you're not her father."

Justin ended the thought for her. "But you can't help wondering if I'm wrong."

She nodded without looking up. "That's about the gist of it. I'm sorry."

"Don't worry about it."

She looked up at last and shrugged. "Anyway," she said. "That's that. Guess all we can do now is wait and see if he finds Linda. But what do we do about the next few days? What about your work? You said you canceled appointments today, but don't you have to turn up tomorrow?''

Justin shrugged. "I can set my own hours, more or less. I do have several obligations, but I'll figure something out. Either postpone, delegate, or even try taking Jenna with me. She sleeps a lot." He sighed with a smile. "At least during the day."

Laura moved to the kitchen, and he followed, smiling when he saw how at home she was in his kitchen by now. It felt nice, although a warning voice reminded him that he'd never before allowed a woman to familiarize herself with his kitchen. "I'll cook this time," she said, rummaging in his fridge. "I make a mean pasta. Where do you work? You never told me, except that you're a speech therapist."

"I run a small center for children with dyslexia, speech impediments, those kind of problems. They come to us after school and get help that their school can't afford to give them."

Laura peeked at him from behind the fridge door, a bag of tomatoes in her hand. The incredulity on her face was pretty obvious. He couldn't help smiling. "Doesn't go with the motorbike, again, huh?"

She was quick to recover, and started chopping celery. "Well, now that I think about it, it probably does. I bet the kids think you're really cool. You run the center? How did that happen?"

He gave her the short version of his adult life. "I got involved in a dot-com adventure when I was barely twenty, and was lucky enough to jump off the wagon at the right time. It paid for college, and I could set up a fund to finance the children's center. So far, it's working out great. A steady, flexible job for me, assistance for the kids.''

She shook her head. ''You spent all your money on a charity project? It didn't occur to you to buy a fleet of motorcycles and a mansion instead?''

Justin grinned. ''I didn't spend everything. Besides, I can only ride one bike at a time.''

''Why speech therapy? Did you stutter as a kid, or something?''

He laughed at her instant guess. ''I know. Terribly transparent, aren't I?''

Laura tucked a stray curl behind her ear, looking flustered for some reason. She also looked beautiful, and temptation simply became too much.

He walked closer, trapping her against the counter. He removed the knife from her hand and turned her around, looping her arms around his neck. She looked startled, but didn't object. In fact, she moved even closer.

Good.

After today, she owed him a kiss. He was going to collect.

The kiss was soft as new fallen snow, but a lot warmer. It seemed like something she'd been waiting for forever. He touched her face, threaded his fingers through her hair and smiled, before kissing her again. This time it wasn't as soft, but the warmth increased, and spread until it cocooned them in a private, safe universe.

Private. Safe. Both of those words applied to her life as a single career woman. They did not apply to a fling with her neighbor. What was she thinking?

She pulled her head back, breaking the kiss long before it had run its course. Justin looked at her, a question in his eyes. She wasn't sure she had the answer he was looking for.

"We're both tired," she croaked, an explanation of nothing. Her arms were still around his neck, and she wasn't in a hurry to move away, but that didn't mean she couldn't set the record straight—that this had been a mistake. "This wouldn't have happened if we weren't both so tired and stressed out."

"You're right," Justin agreed, threading his fingers into the contained tresses of her hair and pushing until her head lay against his shoulder. "When I'm tired, I always look for a workaholic lawyer to kiss. It heals anything."

She couldn't help but grin. She was also far too weak to even raise her head and move away. His breath caressed her temple as he spoke. "Kiss and make it better. Kids have the right idea."

"It must be an inborn instinct." Somewhere, she found the strength to raise her head from his shoulder and take a step back. There. That was better. Wasn't it?

"I like instincts."

Was his face closer again? She squinted to measure the distance. Yep. The ten-inch distance between his face and hers had shrunk to two inches, maximum. She had a terrific view of those eyes now. They weren't just brown, they glinted with dark shades of gold, and they were just as dangerous up close, dark tantalizing pools a girl wanted to throw herself in and stay long past closing time.

"You do?" Was that her voice? That whisper that had an uncomfortable amount of "breathless" in it? Nope. Couldn't be. That voice was begging him to kiss her again, and she wouldn't repeat an act that had been born of pure exhaustion.

"Yeah. They lead to the most interesting situations."

"Like becoming a surrogate parent for a child of unknown origins?"

"Mmm." His arm slipped over her shoulders, and his hand started toying with her hair again. "How long is your hair when it's not in chains?"

"Too long. I should have it cut. It isn't practical."

"Not yet. I want to see it loose first."

But he didn't free it. Which was smart, given their circumstances. But disappointing, nevertheless. Even with the promise of "not yet."

She sighed and pulled away. As tempting as this was, it wasn't a good idea. Things were too complicated right now. "I guess I should finish cooking so I can get to sleep soon. Otherwise I'll fall asleep on my desk tomorrow. The two of you will be okay tonight?"

Reluctantly he let go of her hair. "Yes. We'll be fine."

CHAPTER SIX

THURSDAY, Laura came home at five to find Justin's apartment empty. Frowning, she double-checked all the rooms, and was just beginning her descent into full-blown panic when the front door opened and the low sound of Justin chatting with the baby drifted into the apartment.

Justin looked startled to see her, but greeted her with a bone-melting smile. He was also out of breath, as if he'd been running, and that T-shirt didn't help the consistency of her bones any. In her borrowed stroller, Jenna was being very vocal, waving her arms as she tried out new versions of her trademark noise.

"Hi! Home again? So early?" He glanced at his watch and grinned at her. "This is scary. Can the empire of Young & Warren really continue their course in the world of law without you at the helm?"

Laura grabbed Jenna for a kiss, then put her down in her corner of the sofa. She waved a toy in front of the child until she managed to grab a hold of it. "Yeah, apparently they can. Amazing, isn't it? I'm beginning to think they can do without me stuck to the photocopier or in the filing room until midnight."

"The photocopier? They have you at work as a secretary?"

"Not exactly. It's not something I'm assigned to do. There's just a lot of work to be done. So I do it."

His smile was crooked. "More than your share, it sounds like."

She shrugged. "Probably. I don't think anyone has even noticed that I leave at normal time recently."

That had been surprising. So was the discovery that she was looking forward to getting home, even though nothing more exciting than the daily routine with Jenna—and the daily struggle against Justin's attempts to feed her fattening deserts—awaited her.

The three of them had spent the evenings together, the baby spending the first night with Justin, the second with Laura, and the third with both of them falling asleep on either side of her after a particularly exhausting evening. It had been a sweet morning, Laura thought with a sigh, waking up to find the baby cuddled up against them, thumb in mouth, and Justin fast asleep on the other side of the bed.

She'd ogled for probably half an hour before Jenna had woken him up.

"Harris just called me on the cell phone, and said he was on his way," Justin told her, a worried frown replacing the grin on his face. "Which is why the two of us jogged all the way from work. He has news for us."

Laura felt her heart start to race. "He's found her mother?"

Justin nodded, and at the same time, the doorbell rang. "I'll get it," Laura said, rushing to the door.

"I have a name for you." Mr. Harris said, trampling into the living room. Justin just managed to snatch the baby off the sofa before the PI sat down on her. "Oops. Didn't see her," he cackled. "So much for my powers of observation, huh?"

"Hmm." Justin muttered. He put the baby on her blanket on the floor, well away from the route the good detective might take on his way out of the apartment. "What have you got for us, Mr. Harris?" he asked.

"A name. An address. I've found that woman." He paused, drawing out his moment of glory. "It wasn't easy, but I managed to track her down. Her name is Linda Hope Fielding." He sneered at Justin. "The name fits, the fingerprints fit. That's your child's mother. Any bells ringing yet?"

Justin shrugged.

Mr. Harris dragged a file from his briefcase and looked down at it. "Linda Hope Fielding is forty-two years old, black hair, blue eyes, five-four, one hundred twenty pounds."

"I see."

Mr. Harris seemed annoyed at Justin's refusal to be baited. He dropped the file on the coffee table and stood up. "Well, you may know her or not, but that's the Linda who's been touching your window and that letter. All the information I found is in that file."

Laura grabbed the file and flipped through the few pages.

"You have her current address?" Justin asked, as he walked to Laura's side and peered over her shoulder at the documents. "You're sure she's living there now?"

Mr. Harris grinned. "I wouldn't worry. She's not going far. At least not for the next fifteen to twenty years."

"Oh…" Laura breathed, as she saw the woman's address.

Mr. Harris nodded. "That's right. She's in county jail. She's been wanted for several years, but turned herself in on Monday. That's why it took me so long to find her, her location wasn't in the system when I first checked. It's all in there.''

Laura dropped the file abruptly on the table and almost ran to Jenna. She picked her up and held her close. ''It's okay,'' she whispered into the child's ear. ''Don't worry. Everything will be okay.''

''Did you say she'd been wanted for several years?'' Justin swore, moving closer to Laura and the child. He put his arm over Laura's shoulder, and cradled Jenna's cheek in his hand. ''What's she in for?''

''Larceny. She's a burglar. Apparently she's quite the celebrity among burglars, famous for robbing mansions. She's expected to get minimum fifteen years now.'' He snickered. ''She made the mistake of robbing the governor's home. A bold move, but a foolish one, especially since she managed to leave a fingerprint. Didn't count on them dusting the front gate, I suppose.''

Justin thanked the PI, who left a hefty bill behind, and followed him to the door. Laura sat down on the sofa, hugging Jenna tight. ''A mother who'll be in prison all her childhood. Oh, no. This is worse than we thought.''

''Is it?''

''Well, worse than I thought.''

''Of course. You thought it was an ex-girlfriend of mine, punishing me for not paying child support.''

Laura winced. ''Sorry, Justin. Poor kid. But why would this woman think you're the father of her baby?''

Justin sat down next to her, and they both huddled over the child, as if that would protect her from whatever the future would bring. ''I have no idea, Laura. We should find out as soon as we can talk to Linda. We'll have to hope her father is capable of taking care of her. Her mother obviously thought so, since she tried to leave her with him.''

''What do we do now?''

''We have to contact Linda. We have to let her know her baby is okay, but in the wrong hands. She'll be able to tell us about the father, or other relatives Jenna has.''

''What then? We turn the baby over to the father?''

''We have no choice, do we? It's either her father, if he's capable, or the authorities.'' He flipped through the small file Mr. Harris had left. ''The phone number at the jail is here,'' he said. ''What do you think? Do we try calling her?''

Laura shook her head. ''No. We don't know what kind of phone facilities they have. This is too personal for a phone call. We have to go visit her.''

Getting permission to see Linda took time and effort. Visiting hours were Saturdays only. Although those rules were bendable in special cases, Justin's usual paranoia about Jenna being taken away meant that they couldn't tell the jail authorities their reasons. Getting permission for an unscheduled visit ''just because'' wasn't going to work, even with Laura's connections.

But Saturday arrived soon enough, and Laura's mother—who'd received a detailed report from Steve on the facts of the case—came by her apartment to watch the baby.

Laura didn't feel good about leaving Jenna behind. She hovered over her mother and the little girl, who seemed quite happy with her temporary grandma. ''Are you sure you'll be okay?''

Her mother rolled her eyes. "Laura, I raised you and your brothers. I have four grandsons. I think I can take care of one baby for a couple of hours. Now, go!"

Laura raised her hands and backed away. "Okay, okay. I'm going. Just need to change first."

"You look fine," Justin said. "Let's just go. Isn't she looking fine, Beth?"

Beth looked her up and down. "Well…"

Laura looked down at herself. She was wearing the jeans and T-shirt she'd pulled on this morning, both bearing the marks of Jenna's breakfast. She looked fine, did she? She sent Justin a dark look. "Are you kidding? I'm not even in the close vicinity of 'fine'. There's no way I'm leaving the house looking like this." She entered her bedroom and threw open her closet, hearing Justin follow.

"So what if you have a few stains on your shirts? Shows you've been taking care of the kid. Let's go. It's only half an hour until visiting time."

Laura ignored him and stared at the contents of her closet. "I've only been to the county jail in my professional capacity," she muttered. "How do you dress for a casual visit? Should I wear my lawyer clothes?"

In the mirror above the dresser, she could see Justin lean against the wall, cross his arms and sigh as he stared up at the ceiling. She grinned. It was a posture and a sigh she recognized after having spent almost twenty years of her life living with three males.

"Laura, it doesn't matter. There's no dress code. Replace the T-shirt with something that doesn't smell of strained peas, and you're fine."

"Easy for you to say. All you have to do is wear black, and you look perfect."

Justin glanced at the mirror. He wasn't wearing black, just plain jeans and a camouflage T-shirt. "You're trying to tell me something, right? You mean I should change, too?"

Laura grinned, and grabbed clean trousers and a T-shirt, amused to notice she was choosing the colors so they wouldn't show stains as well. She unzipped her jeans and started to pull them down, then realized maybe they were getting a bit too comfortable with each other. She waved him away. "Justin, go play with Jenna while I change."

Looking back as they made their way toward Laura's car, Laura kept checking for her mother's frantic wave in the window, calling them back to Jenna's side.

No such luck. She reached her car with a sigh, and blinked. Either it had changed color and type, or…

"That's not my car."

Justin glanced in all directions, hand shading his eyes. "You're right. Yours isn't this clean. Where did you leave it?"

"Right here! I remember distinctly."

"Are you sure?"

"I'm sure." Her voice was rising in hysteria. "It's been stolen! I always leave it here if this place is empty. And it was yesterday. I remember it clearly."

"You didn't leave the keys in there, did you?"

"Of course not." She spun around, doing the same inventory of the surroundings that Justin had just done. "I don't believe this! Someone stole my car!"

Justin had whipped out his cell phone when she remembered. She grabbed his wrist to stop him from calling the police. "Uh…wait."

Justin paused, waiting for her to explain. "It wasn't stolen," she explained, embarrassed. "It's with Steve. He has my spare keys. He was going to pick it up to repair it. I forgot."

Justin stared at her before putting the phone back in his pocket. "You're a bit quick to jump to conclusions, aren't you?" he said with a lopsided grin. "Someone broke into your apartment, someone stole your car…"

"Call a taxi, will you?" Laura grumbled. "And someone did break into my apartment, remember? First a cat, then a baby."

Justin put his arm over her shoulders and rubbed his hand up and down her arm as he steered her back toward the house. "Well, the not-stolen car isn't a problem. We'll take my bike."

"What? No. No way." She pulled away to object to the idea—and because close proximity to Justin tended to make her knees weak—but he just grabbed a hold of her hand instead and pulled her onward.

"It'll be fun."

"Justin Bane, listen to me." She dug her heels in and her shoes scraped the pavement for a few feet until he was forced to turn around and look at her. She worked her hand loose of his grasp and articulated every word carefully. "I'm not riding that motorcycle."

"Why not? We need to get to the jail," he added reasonably.

Laura desperately cast around for excuses. She'd rather ride the stuffed train or a bus without air-conditioning than get up on that crazy mechanical monster they called a motorcycle. "I can't. I don't have a helmet."

"No problem." He tightened his grab on her hand and kept going. "I have a spare one for passengers. You can borrow that one."

Hah! A spare one for "passengers." No doubt filled with hairs from all his ex-girlfriends. She'd be damned if she put that one on. "I don't wear strangers' helmets. It's unhygienic." He was still dragging her toward the bike, his hand warm and tight around hers. "Justin, for you, this may be a walking pace. For me it's a running pace. Now, call a taxi, please."

"Oh. Sorry." He slowed down, and stopped, pushing the leather jacket out of the way as he put his hands on his hips and stared at her. "Are you serious? You're too scared to ride on the bike with me?"

"I'm not scared. I just don't want to." She held out her hand for his phone. "Either call a taxi, or give me the phone so I can do it."

He lifted the phone out of his pocket, but held it out of her reach. "You promise you'll consider it? The bike ride? It would be fun."

"Sure." She held her hand out for the phone. "I'll consider it."

The same day she'd consider taking up crocodile wrestling.

Laura had been to prisons before, including the county jail, but it felt different to be there as a visitor, instead of as a lawyer. Justin didn't seem troubled, and she wondered for a moment how familiar he was with this environment.

Once they reached the large hall that served as visiting quarters, a guard pointed them toward Linda. She matched Mr. Harris's description. She was thin, her face still tanned from the outside world, but she looked tired and depressed as she sat there, elbows resting on the table as she stared in the direction of the in-coming flood of visitors.

If any doubts remained in Laura's head, they were put to rest when there was no flash of recognition in Linda's eyes when they shook her hand. Laura introduced herself, but Justin didn't. Linda didn't question who he was. She just nodded at them both, a look of boredom masking curiosity.

Laura leaned over the desk and beamed her professional smile. "Ms. Fielding, you're probably wondering who we are and why we're here."

Linda shrugged.

Laura glanced at Justin to check if he was in the mood for doing the talking.

Apparently not.

"We're here about your daughter, Jenna."

"Jenna?" That got Linda's attention, and she sat up straight in her chair, leaning toward them.

"I live at 23 Oak Street. You broke into my apartment and left your daughter on my bed."

Linda's eyes narrowed, and she looked Laura up and down. "That's right. I recognize you now. You're the new bimbo."

"I'm not a..." She stopped herself, and looked at

Justin for guidance. No help there. He was staring at Linda without blinking. "Ms. Fielding…" she started.

"Call me Linda. If you're going to be raising my daughter, we might as well be on first-name basis." Linda grabbed a cigarette from her breast pocket and lit it with a match. She drew a deep breath and blew the smoke to the side. "Thank God for cigarettes. That's the only positive thing about having to leave my child with you. I could start smoking again. It was a difficult year without them."

"Linda, the fact is, you made a mistake. I'm the wrong bimbo." She cursed herself. Where had her glib tongue run off to? "I mean, I live alone in that apartment. Jenna's father does not live there."

"He does live there. His name was in the phone book. And I asked a neighbor. Apartment 3C."

Laura's apartment. "What's the name of your daughter's father? You wrote Justin on the note—what is his last name?"

"Bane. His name is Justin Bane."

Laura looked at Justin who hadn't moved since they'd sat down. His expression hadn't changed. "Linda, Justin Bane lives in apartment 3B. And he says he's never heard of you. He says he couldn't possibly be the baby's father."

Linda's face reddened in anger. "He's lying. He knows only too well he's the father of my child. His name is on the birth certificate, and I contacted him after she was born. He knows very well he has a daughter."

Laura stared at the woman. "Linda, this is Justin Bane." She pointed at him. "Are you still saying he is the father of your baby?"

"What?" Linda almost dropped her cigarette. "He's not Justin Bane. Do I look like a cradle robber?" She blew smoke in the air and stared at Justin. "He'll be ripe in about ten years, but I wouldn't touch him until then."

Under other circumstances, Laura would have laughed, but there didn't seem to be anything funny about this situation. Not when there was an innocent infant with an uncertain future waiting back home. "Okay. If this is not the father of your baby, then it's obvious that you left your child in the wrong apartment."

Linda stabbed out her half-finished cigarette, looking worried now. "He was the only Justin Bane in the phone book. I was sure it was him. Where is Jenna? Is she okay?"

"Jenna is fine," Laura assured her. "Don't worry. We've been taking good care of her."

"How did you find me?"

"We hired a private investigator. He found your fingerprints on my window, and on the letter."

Linda's smile was wry. "Of course. Fingerprints."

Laura fetched a notepad and a pen from her pocket. "Linda, we need to find her father. What can you tell us about your Justin Bane?"

"When we met, he was living on the other side of the city. He's older than this one. By ten or twenty years, I'm not sure how old he is."

"What does he do for a living?"

Linda shrugged. "This and that. He's good at making money out of nothing." She reclaimed her cigarette from the ashtray and tried to repair the damage done to the end. "And vice versa, but I'm hoping that will change now that he's a father."

A violent expletive boomed through the air. Both women twisted their heads to look at Justin. He was staring up at the ceiling with a thunderstruck expression, his features frozen in a mask of astonished rage.

"What's wrong, Justin?" Laura asked, reaching out to touch his arm.

Justin shook his head. He leaned forward and slammed a palm on the table. "I don't believe it. But of course that's it. How come it didn't occur to me sooner?"

"What?" the two women asked in unison.

"My father," Justin growled. "I haven't seen him since I was a child, but I share a name with my father." He looked at Laura. "Jenna must be my father's child. She must be...my sister."

Linda gasped in surprise, but then smiled for the first time. "My little Jenna has a big brother?"

Justin seemed almost paralyzed now, staring down at the table in shock. Laura turned back to Linda, giving him time to compose himself. "That solves that mystery. But why did you leave the baby behind? We're told that you turned yourself in."

Linda shook her head and shrugged. "There was no choice. I've been on the run for years. It's no life for a child. I counted on Justin—senior," she amended, nodding at Justin. "He's managed to stay out of prison so far, and he has been doing well lately. I have no family of my own."

"How could you trust him with Jenna?" Justin broke

in. "If you know that man, you'll know he has no sense of responsibility. None at all."

"He's her father," Linda said stubbornly. "He'll take care of her."

Justin slumped in his seat, hands moving in a gesture of defeat. "Yes. Of course he will. Just like he took care of me and Ben."

"Maybe your father has changed, Justin," Laura said. "It's been a long time. Linda, do you really trust him with your baby?"

Linda bit her lip in doubt. "He's her father," she repeated once more. "He may not be a good father, but it's better than no family at all. Better than a mother who can't send her to school or take her to the hospital because she's wanted by the police. I had no choice."

"Jenna will most likely be an adult when you get out," Laura said.

Linda nodded. "I know. I might be there just in time for her high school graduation."

Justin leaned toward Linda, his eyes again blazing with anger and fear. "Linda, my father is not capable of taking care of a baby. He wasn't when I was a child, and I very much doubt he is now. My brother and I were removed from his care after several months of serious neglect. We can't let that happen to Jenna." He repeated the sentence for emphasis. "We can't let that happen to Jenna. My little brother, Ben, died because he had a lousy father. Don't let that happen to your baby. You can't let him have her."

Linda had turned pale as the force of Justin's words sank in. "I didn't know...I don't know Justin very well, but after I had tracked him—you—down, I was sure she'd be safe. I saw the nice neighborhood, and the neat apartment building, the park around the corner.'' Her gaze flickered to Laura for an instant. ''And the bimbo seemed nice too. I was sure she'd be safe, that she'd be better off than with me. Jenna doesn't have anyone except her father. There was no one else I could turn to with her. If I'd known he was so untrustworthy, I wouldn't have... Oh, God.''

Justin's universe was in chaos. He had a sister, an infant sibling again. The little baby girl he'd spent a week looking after, feeding and bathing and rocking off to sleep, was his sister.

He drew in a breath and found that he was trembling. No wonder he'd felt a bond with Jenna, felt this strong urge to protect and take care of her, this irrepressible driving need to make sure nothing happened to her. On an unconscious level he must have recognized her.

Linda was now rocking back and forth, frantic worry freezing her features. Through the shock, Justin felt an unexpected compassion toward his sister's mother. He reached out and touched her hand. ''Don't worry, Linda. Jenna will be safe. She's my sister, I'll make sure she'll be safe.''

Linda's terrified eyes didn't flicker as her gaze bored into his. ''How? How can you do that? She has no one. No one at all.''

Justin didn't think. The words just came out. ''She has me. Will you let me take care of her?''

Linda stared at Justin for a long time, doubt and hope most visible among the many emotions crossing over her face. "I don't know…" she said at last. "Can I talk to the bimbo alone?"

"Her name is Laura," Justin said tiredly, and stood up. He didn't bother to wonder why Linda wanted to talk to Laura alone about the possibility of him taking care of his sister. He walked to the other end of the room and waited, watching the two women talk in earnest, their heads bent together over the middle of the table.

The waiting wasn't a chore. There was plenty to think about. He had his whole life, his whole outlook on the universe to dismantle and put back together again.

He had a sister. For the first time since Ben had died, he wasn't alone in the world. The wonder was almost equal to the weight of responsibility that came with it.

Eventually they gestured for him to return.

Judging by the determined look on her face, Linda's mind seemed to be made up, but he had no idea in which direction her decision had fallen. He sat down, and looked between the two women. "Well?"

"You'd have to adopt her formally," Linda said. "Would you do that?"

"Adopt her? Not simply get custody of her?"

Linda shook her head. "No. It has to be a permanent adoption. So she'll be safe for sure. For good. So no one will be able to take her away from you. Not your father, nobody. Make it all official and permanent. She'll be your adopted daughter."

Justin digested that. "Okay. I'll adopt her." Linda's request was a surprise, and he didn't quite know how to interpret it. "You trust me?" he settled for asking, hoping for some sort of explanation.

Linda glanced at Laura. "Yes. I've talked to your

bim…to Laura. She trusts you to raise Jenna. She's been good to my daughter. I trust her judgment.''

"I'll take good care of her.''

Linda was wringing her hands. "But can you tell me why you want to do this? You're a single man. Why would you want a baby?''

"She's my sister. We're family. If she can't be with her parents, she belongs with me, rather than with strangers.''

Linda leaned backward and fished another cigarette out of her pocket. "You know, I spent several weeks with Just. Jenna's father. Your father. He never even mentioned you. It doesn't look like blood means much in your family.''

"I'm not my father. My sister means a lot to me,'' Justin said. "You won't be able to be there for her. I can take good care of her.''

Linda nodded. "Just bring me the papers to sign. As soon as possible. I want all this settled and over with. I want Jenna safe.''

Justin saw compassion burn in Laura's face. She reached out to touch Linda's hand. "Don't worry. She'll be taken great care of. Justin is the best big brother anyone could have. He'll make an excellent foster father.''

Linda looked up, tears damping her eyes. "He'd better. Now go home to Jenna, and get everything in motion. And then bring me the damn papers. And hurry.''

"We will,'' Justin said, reaching out to shake hands with his sister's mother. "Thank you.'' They stood up, as the guard was at the door, signaling them that their time was over. "We'll let you know what happens, Linda.''

She nodded. "Kiss my daughter from me."

"We will," Laura whispered, and they turned to leave.

"Justin?"

Justin turned around to face her again. Linda had stood up, and looked very small, standing there in her jail clothes. "Yes?"

"When my daughter asks, you can tell her that I stole from the rich and gave to the poor. You can tell her I was a female Robin Hood."

"You gave to the poor?" Justin asked skeptically.

"Yes." Linda grinned sadly at him. "Me."

CHAPTER SEVEN

"IMAGINE," Laura muttered, in the back of the taxi on the way home, thinking about little Jenna. "Imagine having parents who can't look after you, and nobody else in the world. Without you, she'd have no one."

"I don't know Laura, that really stretches my power of imagination," Justin growled. Laura started. She'd forgotten that Justin's situation had been the same. "Poor kid," Justin continued. "Not exactly stellar genes she's starting out with."

Laura grabbed his hand, not sure if she meant to comfort or reprimand. "Don't talk like that, Justin."

"Why not? I share her genes. We're two peas in a pod, and we both share whatever it was that made our father the jerk that he is." He was staring out the window, jaw clenched. "Not a great starting ground for a kid."

"You make your own fate," Laura objected. "Scientists may be finding links to just about everything in our genes, but I strongly believe in free will." She tightened her grip on his wrist, and shook him. "You're nothing like your father, Justin. Nothing at all! And neither is Jenna."

A small smile broke through the dark cloud of Justin's face. "She's not even four months old, Laura. You can already tell?"

"Yes." She heard her voice soften just at the mention

111

of the little girl. "She's an angel. And she's a lot like you."

Justin's smile was bittersweet as he glanced at her at last. "Thank you. I can only take that as a compliment. Tell me, what did you two talk about while I was dismissed?"

"You. She wanted to know what kind of a man you were, and how you took care of Jenna, how you felt about her, if you got impatient when she cried, that sort of thing."

"Funny that she wants to research me, but intended to dump her on her father without even a word."

"I know. She seems to have been fixated on his biological fatherhood, as if that would ensure he'd take care of her. She does love Jenna deeply. She's sacrificing a lot for her."

"Jenna deserves sacrifices."

Laura smiled at him. "She's getting plenty of them." She glanced at her watch. "Look, my mother isn't expecting us back for another hour. Why don't we stop somewhere for lunch and plan the next step?"

"I'd really like to get home to see Jenna as soon as possible."

"Okay." She could understand that he was eager to see his sister again, to hold her and realize that they were family. "You know, it would help your case if we made sure you had your father's consent to adopt Jenna," she pointed out. "His name is on her birth certificate. Do you think he'll agree?"

Justin shook his head. "I have no idea. I haven't met him since I was five years old."

Jenna was sleeping in Laura's bed when they got back. Justin vanished immediately inside the bedroom.

Laura sat down with her mother in the kitchen for a cup of coffee, sensing that he needed to be alone with his sister. She told her mother the whole story twice, drank three cups of coffee and heard every possible grandchild story before she decided she'd have to check on Justin.

The baby was awake in the middle of the bed, lying quietly with arms and legs flailing, a toy in one hand. Justin was beside her, his head propped up on a hand, one finger in her fist.

Laura stroked the baby's cheek and sat down next to Justin. "Hi," she said quietly. "Getting to know each other?"

"Yeah. She's really my sister." There was wonder in his voice, and none of the darkness from before, when he'd talked about the heritage he shared with his sister. "Isn't it amazing?"

She chuckled. "Yes. Not many men your age have an infant brother or sister."

Justin kept looking at his sister. He looked tired, but the determination in his eyes showed that the weight of the task he was about to undertake was a challenge, not a burden.

"Scared?" she asked.

Justin glanced up at her, silent for a moment before shrugging in a gesture of helplessness. "Of course. I don't know if I can take care of her well enough."

"I suppose a parent can never know that."

"Oh, God." Justin jumped to his feet and crossed to the window. He opened it, and leaned out. "I need oxygen. Oh, God. I'm a parent. I need to be a father to my sister. How am I going to do this?"

"You'll do fine, Justin. You've done fine so far."

''That's not the same. You were there to help me. And it was just temporary. I can't take care of a baby.''

''Of course you can. You've been doing that for a week now. You've done great.''

Justin shook his head, still leaning out the window as if collecting oxygen fresh from the trees outside. ''You don't understand. My little brother, Ben. I couldn't take care of him.''

''Your little brother? The one who died as an infant?''

''Yes. I was supposed to look after him. Then he got pneumonia, and he died. I probably didn't keep him warm enough. I could have gone to the neighbors and asked for help. I should have done something. I might have saved Ben if I'd...'' He rubbed his face with his hands. ''If I'd done something.''

Laura frowned, sympathizing with his grief, but not understanding the guilt. ''Didn't you say you were just a child when Ben died?''

''I was five.''

''You can't seriously think it's your fault.''

''No,'' Justin pushed himself away from the window, rejecting her words with a whole body movement. ''Not rationally. But the thought of taking care of a child...raising a child...I mean, diapers are the easy bits. Then there are birthday parties for twenty little girls. PTA meetings. Birds and bees discussion. Then she'll grow up. She'll be a teenager. I'll have to beat boys away from the door. There is no way I'm allowing her to date until she's twenty-five. Oh, God.'' He collapsed into a chair as if he couldn't bear the weight of impending fatherhood anymore. ''I can't do this. I have to do this. I can't. I must.''

"Justin, are you in the midst of developing a multiple personality or are you just having a panic attack?"

Her lame joke got a small smile, but it disappeared quickly. "I've always been so careful," he continued, so slumped that it was a wonder he didn't sink through the chair. "So careful that there was never a moment's doubt that she could be my kid, remember? I've avoided commitment, avoided relationships, so determined never to bring children into this world when I wasn't capable of giving them all they need. And now I'm going to be a father." His brows were heavy as he stared at his sister. "It's the ultimate irony."

"Don't get too carried away," she warned him. "We don't even know yet if you'll get to adopt her. We have to talk to your father, and to the authorities. It's far from settled."

"What do you mean?" He stared at her like an angry tiger. "What's there to settle? Neither of her parents are capable of looking after her. I'm her brother, her only relative. Of course it's settled."

"We need to see your father. Do you have any idea where he is?"

"No."

"Lucky we have Mr. Harris."

Justin acknowledged her suggestion with a nod. "I'll talk to him." He looked down at Jenna, who had succumbed to sleep. "You know, it makes sense that I'm her brother," he mused. "Her eyes are blue now, but she has the same shape of eyes as I do, and I wouldn't be surprised if hers turned brown later." He stroked the child's eyebrow with a finger. "Hi, Jenna," he whispered. "What do you know, you have a big brother almost old enough to be your grandfather."

"Come on. You'd have to have started awfully early to be her grandfather," Laura found herself compelled to argue.

Justin grinned. "Wouldn't be far off, if I'd followed the family tradition. I'm thirty-one. My father is forty-seven."

"*Forty-seven?* You mean he was sixteen when you were born?"

"Yep."

"Wow. How old was your mother?"

"Fifteen." Justin was still preoccupied, his gaze on his sister almost reverent. "We should be getting home. On the other side of the wall. And I should call Harris as soon as possible. After that, we start the adoption process."

"Justin...are you sure this is what you want? Have you thought this through?"

"Thought what through?"

"Being a single parent isn't a picnic. Just look at us— one week, and we're exhausted. And there are two of us. With only you to care for her, the workload is double. You're taking on a lifetime commitment here."

"I know. And I'm terrified. But I don't have a choice, do I? My sister has no one else." His voice was defensive, his eyes almost angry.

"I'm not trying to dissuade you. I just want to point out the potential problems so there will be fewer surprises. For example, how are you going to manage working and raising an infant?"

"I don't know." Justin's angry manner faded as he sat down again, next to his sister. "But I'll manage. We'll adapt. Single mothers manage, why shouldn't I? And I'm lucky in that my job is relatively flexible. While

I don't have daycare, I might even be able to bring her with me most of the time. We'll be fine. We'll be great.''

Struck by his determination, Laura slid down next to brother and sister, her hand on Justin's shoulder. "You don't think your father will take responsibility for her?"

"I would be very surprised to hear that my father had changed. I'm not letting him get away with anything this time. If he wants to take her, I'll go to the police. After what happened with me and Ben, he must have a record of criminal negligence. They'll never allow him to keep her."

"What does he do? Is he working?"

"I don't know. I think he does whatever it takes to get by. He used to have some success gambling. That was his main occupation last time I knew."

"You mean he's a professional gambler?"

Justin shrugged. "That was what my case file said. I wouldn't know. From what I read, it sounded like he does fine while his luck holds. If he manages to stop when he's ahead, he blows his winnings on long drunken binges. He is also a professional thief, and an alcoholic, and a general manipulator of anyone who might part with some money, especially if they're female."

"You got to read your case file back then?"

"I stole it. I was curious."

"Guess I can understand that. And your mother?"

"My mother was just a kid. She had me at fifteen, and my brother at nineteen. She died a few months after my brother was born. Car accident. I hardly remember her at all."

"What happened to you then?"

"We were split up. Then Ben died, and I was put in

foster care. There was at least one family who wanted to adopt me shortly after. But my father prevented it.''

''He wanted you with him?''

Justin snorted. ''Hardly. I don't know why, but he didn't want me to have a real family. So I went to a series of temporary foster homes. And orphanages in between. I never saw him again, but he still had the power to hold up the process until the family who wanted to adopt me gave up.''

''When did your brother die?''

''He was only ten months old. I don't even have a picture of him. But I remember his eyes. They looked like Jenna's eyes. And he loved to gnaw on my knuckles when he was teething.'' He laughed without humor. ''No doubt I passed a lot of germs onto him.''

''You passed on a lot of love to him. And you'll do the same for Jenna.''

His eyes were so sad that she longed to reach out and comfort him. ''Love isn't always enough, Laura.''

''It's a good start,'' she whispered.

''Justin?'' Laura's mother stood in the door, motioning toward him. ''Would you talk to me for a second?''

Suspicious, Laura stood up to follow Justin out of the room, but her mother winked and shut the door in her face. ''I'll return him in a moment,'' she called. Laura sat down next to the baby, wondering what her mother was up to.

She interrogated Justin as soon as her mother had left, but all he offered was a noncommittal reply about her mother wanting advice on her herb garden.

''Justin, for one thing: my mother doesn't have a herb garden. Second, what do you know about herb gardens?''

Justin glanced at her, surprised. "Are you sure? She says she has a herb garden right outside the kitchen entrance."

Laura thought. "Oh. I suppose that's possible. I got her a book on herb gardens for Christmas last year, since she'd talked about it every now and then. I never asked if she'd used it."

"Guess she wasn't exaggerating when she said they never saw you anymore. And haven't you seen my window boxes?"

"Excuse me? You grow herbs in window boxes?"

Justin nodded. "I think it's fun. And your mother tells me she grows a lot of them in her garden.

"Oh. I suppose I really should visit them more often."

"Tomorrow is Sunday," Justin pointed out. "She suggested we drop in. You can praise her parsley before winter gets it."

"We? You know, if they see much more of you, they'll be booking the church," Laura warned him.

Justin grinned. "Let them. I can use it for Jenna's christening. She hasn't been christened yet. I'm thinking about asking Linda if she agrees to naming her Jennifer Patricia."

Laura laughed. "So she'd be a Pat after all? That's cute. Do you think Linda's going to stay in Jenna's life?"

"I don't know. I don't know what Linda wants and I don't know what's good for Jenna. We'll just have to stumble our way through this the best we can."

Knowing that now Justin's "we" only referred to him and Jenna, Laura felt left out. It wasn't logical, she told herself, irritated at her own feelings. This wasn't about her. She would help Justin and Jenna to adjust, the best she could, then slowly withdraw from their family.

But not just yet. They needed her, she told herself.

Mr. Harris left Justin's apartment, shaking his head. "First the mother, now the father," he was muttering when the door closed after him.

Justin grimaced. "Okay, he's not the friendliest guy around, but he does give quick results," he pointed out. Laura nodded, as she finished changing Jenna's diaper and put her in one of the dresses Justin had bought on an impulse yesterday. She was no longer wearing only green and white. No, Justin had kept his promise and now the baby wore honest-to-God pink, complete with a bow, and wouldn't have been mistaken for a boy even with action figures in both hands as well as a blue diaper.

"She doesn't have enough hair for a bow," Laura complained, trying to fit the length of cloth around the wispy black curls. Justin took over, fiddling with his sister's hair, until the pink bow was indeed stuck to her head. It wasn't perfect, but at least she didn't look anything like a "Patrick" anymore.

"There!" he said, satisfied. "Now you're ready for that visit to Laura's mother."

"Visit to my mother?" Laura parroted. "Now? Why?"

"She asked us over yesterday, remember? An afternoon in the garden. Showing us her herb garden. Might be Jenna's only chance to get grass between her toes until next summer."

"When did she ask you? When she dragged you out of the room and closed the door on my face?" What was her mother up to? Laura grimaced at herself. She knew very well what her mother was up to. "Guess that means you two are invited, and I'm not."

"Don't be silly. She just wants to show me—"

"The herb garden," Laura interrupted. "I know."

The phone rang, and Justin grabbed it, Jenna still in his arms. "Hi, Steve. Yes, she's here." He passed the phone to Laura. "It's for you."

Now people were calling her at Justin's place. Laura shook her head as she accepted the phone, wondering if her mother had started sewing a wedding gown already.

"Hey, sis," Steve called, obviously on his cell phone. "I'm on my way to Mom's. Want me to pick you all up? I'm driving your car anyway."

"You fixed it already?"

"Of course. Wouldn't be returning it otherwise, would I? The boys can't wait to see Jenna. I'll leave them with Mom first, then pick you up in half an hour, okay?"

"Sure." Laura muttered. Apparently her destiny was to spend today at her mother's house. There wasn't really anything one could do with runaway trains, was there? You just had to hang on and hope for the best.

Her car didn't make a weird sound every time she stepped on the brakes, so Steve got a big hug for his trouble. Jenna's borrowed car seat fit neatly into the middle of the back seat, and the little girl had the two men on either side of her. They talked motorbikes. What else?

As soon as she pulled into her parents' driveway, her mother appeared around the corner of the house and waved to them. "Come on!" she called.

Laura got Jenna out of the car seat, while the men were still talking in a foreign language, and they followed her mother toward the backyard. It was a lovely day, warm with only the slightest hint of a cooling breeze. Laura reminded herself to ask her mother about that herb garden.

"Surprise!" was yelled as soon as they rounded the corner. Tightening her arms around the baby, Laura jumped backward, and might have fallen if Justin hadn't been standing right behind her, his hand going around her shoulders to steady her.

"What's going on?" she breathed, looking around in astonishment.

Conspiracy. Justin had been dragged into one of her mother's conspiracies. Her whole family was there, and they'd strung balloons and confetti along the trees—although, this time of year, the added color was hardly needed.

There was a pile of presents stacked on a table on the porch, and her four nephews were circling it, eyeing the wrapped goodies hungrily. Her father was already busy manning the huge barbecue he only got to use a couple of times every year.

"Oh, Lord. Mom... My birthday isn't until Tuesday, you know."

"I know. Happy birthday." Her mother squeezed the air out of her and kissed both her cheeks. "On Tuesday, you'll be too busy. Well, you may be too busy for birthdays, but birthdays are not too busy for you."

Laura chuckled, knowing better than to try to translate that cryptic remark. She knelt down to hug her nephews, four blond and energetic boys, ranging from two to five years old. She hadn't seen them a lot since she started working so much, and they actually seemed bigger.

"Boys," Laura's mother said, her hand on Justin's

arm. "This is Justin. Laura's friend. And this is his baby sister."

The boys abandoned her to gather around Justin and their grandmother, straining their necks to get a look at Jenna. "Wow, she's just like a doll," the oldest one breathed and Laura just managed to catch his hand before he poked Jenna's cheek.

"Aunt Laura, you need to open your presents!" he said, tugging on the hand she had imprisoned. "We've been waiting forever!"

Laura let herself be dragged toward the porch. Feeling slightly faint, she set to work opening her presents with the diligent help of her nephews. She hadn't celebrated her birthday for years, not since starting college.

"There's one more," Justin said, digging in the huge diaper bag, which Laura just now noticed was unusually bulky. Justin's eyes were glinting as he dug up a large parcel and handed it to her. It was a big box, wrapped in red paper with a big white bow. She kissed his cheek, as she had her brothers, tore off the paper and opened the plain cardboard box underneath.

"Oh, no!" she exclaimed in horrified dismay at seeing the contents. "Justin, what are you doing to me?"

"Jenna helped me pick it out," Justin said with an evil grin. "She's to blame for the color."

Laura held up the fire-engine red motorcycle helmet. "My very own helmet. Red. Oh, Lord." She dropped the helmet on the table and with one finger pushed it as far away as she could. She stared at Justin. "How could you do this to me?"

"Laura!" her mother said, horrified at her lack of manners, but Justin calmed her with a grin.

"She's been refusing to try out my bike because she

doesn't have a helmet," he explained. "So I thought I'd solve that problem. I was expecting a lecture about men and manipulation, not shouts of joy, so she's not hurting my feelings."

"But still..." her mother said. "Laura..."

"Well, thank you, Justin," Laura said in her best polite voice. "I love it. The helmet will look great in my trophy collection, right next to my bungee cord, the Everest ice pick and the parachute."

"Good luck, buddy. She has a thing about motorbikes," Steve told Justin. "She refused to try again after she almost killed my Suzy. And she's always been stubborn as hell. You're going to have a hard time convincing her."

"Yeah," Roy chimed in. "Might be easiest just to pick her up and put her there, and take off before she has the chance to escape."

Laura carefully put the helmet back in its box. "See, Justin?" she asked. "This is what my childhood was like." She gave Justin a nasty glare. "You better treat your sister better than they treated me."

"I promise," said Justin solemnly. "No mopeds for Jenna. Just a Harley."

The afternoon passed far too quickly, as Laura got reacquainted with her nephews and the taste of her father's barbecued steak. They were finishing off her mother's trademark pecan pie as a dessert when Justin's cell phone beeped. He excused himself and walked away to take the call.

"It's Harris," he told Laura, when he got back a few minutes later. He was pale. "I have to go."

"What is it? He found your father?"

Justin glanced around, and Laura grabbed his arm and pulled him away for some privacy.

"Yeah. He found him. He's staying at a hotel, and Harris has no idea how long he'll be staying there. So I'm going to see him now." He moved restlessly. "I'd better take Jenna with me."

She nodded. "You get her ready, and I'll pile up my loot."

"You don't have to leave, Laura. It's your birthday party."

"We would have left soon anyway. Don't worry. Go get Jenna."

"I really like Justin," her mother whispered, as they hugged goodbye. "He's a bit reticent, but I think he's a good one. He obviously adores his sister."

Laura smiled. Reticent—well, Justin had been rather silent. He'd seemed overwhelmed by her family. She didn't blame him. They overwhelmed her too, sometimes, and she'd had twenty-five years to get used to them. "Don't read too much into this, Mom. He's my neighbor, and we happened to end up babysitting together for a while. That's all."

"But you like him, don't you?"

Laura stared into her mother's eyes. "Yes, Mom. I like him."

"A lot?"

"A lot," she confirmed, to herself as well as to her mother, looking up with a sigh at Justin lifting one of her nephews out of a tree so the little boy could say goodbye to Jenna.

Yeah. That was the problem. She liked him a lot.

*   *   *

Justin didn't start the car right away. He leaned his head against the headrest, and Laura saw him turn more and more pale.

This wasn't going to be easy on him. She leaned across, and despite the awkward position, put her arms around him. He wasn't very responsive to her hug at first, but she didn't let go. He wasn't used to accepting other people, but he needed her now.

"How long has it been since you've seen your father?" she asked, after a long silence.

"More than twenty-five years." Justin's voice was flat. "I was just five. Hardly remember him. I doubt I'll even recognize him when I see him."

"Did he mistreat you?"

"No. He just ignored us. Left us alone."

"That's one type of mistreatment. You and your brother?"

"Yeah."

"That was after your mother died?"

"Yeah. There wasn't anyone else. And our father didn't…well, let's just say he wasn't a model father. We were taken away from him six months later." Justin shrugged. "He's nothing to me. This won't be a problem. I just have to stay polite and not let him see how much I despise him, until he agrees to let me adopt Jenna."

Laura winced. This wasn't sounding promising. "Do you remember those six months?"

"Yeah. I remember Ben. I don't remember my mother's face, but I'll never forget Ben."

Laura rested her head on his shoulder and tried to draw the tension out of him. She found herself wishing she could make it all better, but knew it wasn't possible. There was no way her hugs could erase the old scars.

But maybe they could comfort for a while.

"I should take you home first," Justin muttered. He turned his head, nuzzling into her neck, and she raised her hand, allowed her fingers to crawl into his hair. His breath was hot against her skin.

"Laura?" he said, the question hollow, but his eyes, hot as he raised his head and looked into hers, so close that their noses touched, were anything but hollow. She tightened her grip on his hair.

"Yes?"

"You're beautiful."

She grinned. "So are you. I told you before—killer eyes."

He grimaced, and she laughed at him.

"I was trying to lead up to a kiss here, not fishing for a compliment," he complained.

"Do I get to come with you to see your father?"

"What's that got to do with the kiss?" Justin asked, his fingers caressing her cheek.

"It could help to have a lawyer with you. And a friend. I can be both. Let me come?"

Justin hesitated. "Why?"

She evaded the question and leaned closer. "Because there might be a kiss in it for you."

There was a smile in Justin's eyes as his arms went around her. "Not an offer I can turn down," he whispered.

"Good," she murmured back, and just as their lips were about to meet she pulled away and moved as far away as the confines of the car would allow.

It wasn't very far. Justin's hand was still on her shoulder. He glared at her. "Hey! Going back on your word? Come back here! We have unfinished business."

"No." She grinned at him. "First the visit, then the kiss." She blew him a finger kiss as a small compensation, hoping to tease another smile out of him. She liked chasing the shadows from his eyes. "Come on. Start the car. Let's go."

Justin gave her an evil look as he started the car. "Okay. But I'm holding you to that kiss. You're not wriggling out of this one."

This was promising. She'd help him face down his father, hopefully get him the permission to adopt his sister. And after that: A kiss.

Yup, she could get through anything for that kind of a reward. She hoped Justin felt the same.

Justin took a deep breath as they stopped outside the door marked 2C in gold letters. The drive had been far too short, the hotel all too easy to find. He wasn't ready to be here.

He raised his hand to knock, but after a moment tucked his fist under his left arm. He sighed, not looking at Laura. He hoped she knew he was glad she was there, and not because she was a lawyer.

But he didn't want to face his father. He really didn't.

Laura slid her hand under his arm and stood closer. He looked down at her and sent her a faint smile. Then he looked at the floor where Jenna was sleeping in her car seat. He had to do this. For her.

He lifted his hand again and knocked firmly on the door.

There was movement from within, then pause which signaled someone looking at them through the peephole. Justin tensed even further as they waited, and Laura's grip on his arm tightened.

"Yeah?" A voice came from within. "What is it?"

Justin opened his mouth, but somehow his practiced introduction had vanished and no words emerged.

"Mr. Bane?" Laura called. "We'd like to talk with you a moment."

"What about?"

"My name is Justin Bane," Justin said, surprised to find his voice steady. "I'm…your son. I need to talk to you."

There was silence for a moment. Then the door was opened.

He recognized him after all, Justin realized. The memory was faint, and the man was a lot older, but there was the definite feeling that they'd met before. He even remembered the name—Just. His father had wanted him to call him Just. He nodded at the man who was his father, in the biological sense if nothing else. This was his link to Jenna. He had to remember that.

"Justin junior?" the older man asked at last. "I'll be damned." He looked down at the car seat where Jenna was sleeping. "And a grandchild?"

"Hello, Just," Justin said levelly. "We'd like to talk to you for a moment."

His father gaze move to Laura. "Your wife?"

"No. This is Laura King. She's a lawyer."

"A lawyer?" Just looked suspicious, but motioned for them to come in, and led the way to a spacious sitting room. "There. Have a seat. What are you here for, boy? Checking out your inheritance?" A laugh accompanied his little joke. "I'm nowhere close to the grave yet, so don't expect anything any time soon."

"You seem to be doing all right," Justin said. "This is an expensive hotel."

His father preened. "Yes. I've done well in the last couple of months. But money comes and goes. That's life."

Laura sat down, but Justin didn't. He left the car seat at his feet, crossed his arms on his chest and looked at his father, determined to get this over with as quickly as possible. "I'm here about Jenna."

"Jenna? Who's Jenna?"

Justin pointed at the child. "That's Jenna. Your daughter."

The older man blinked. He peered at the baby, then away. "Linda's baby. Right. What in the world is she doing with you? Can you believe that Linda demanded money if I wanted the kid to have my name? I had to cough up a thousand. Is her legal name Bane?"

Justin didn't answer his father's last question. "Linda is in jail. The baby has been with me for a while."

"Linda finally got caught, did she? I told her not to be too cocky."

Justin leaned forward, trying to capture his father's attention. "Just, we're here to talk about the baby's future," he said. "Linda has agreed to have the child adopted. All we need is your consent, and you don't have to worry about this any more."

Right. As if their father spent a moment of his life worrying about his children.

"No way. That's my kid. She's not getting adopted."

Justin stared down at the coffee table, resisting his violent impulses as he remembered another adoption his father had vetoed. He was thankful for the calming presence of Laura by his side, and managed to keep his question civilized. "Why not?"

"She's my child. My daughter."

Justin picked up the sleeping child and held her to his chest, making it impossible for his father to look at him without seeing his daughter, too. "Do you mean you want to raise her yourself?"

Just shifted uncomfortably. "Of course not. That's her mother's business. I just mean that she will bloody well keep my name until she gets married."

Hope raised its head. If that was all... "Just, her mother will most likely be in prison for many years. *I* want to adopt her. She'll keep the name. Our name."

"I see." Just stared at him and Jenna for a while, then shrugged. "Well, that's different then, isn't it?" He lit a cigarette and Justin shifted to move out of the cloud of smoke. "Fine with me. You want to raise your sister? What a weird boy you are. You always were."

"How would you know, Just?" he asked calmly. "You never knew me."

"Don't try to make me feel guilty, son. I was a child when you were born. Barely turned twenty when your brother joined us. And then I lost your mother." He was silent for a minute, but Justin didn't want to consider that he might still be grieving for his mother. "I was just a kid myself. How could anyone expect me to take care of two babies?"

"You're not a kid now."

"Nope. Reckon I'm turning middle-aged." He gave a wink. "Yet I produced a child."

"Do I get your permission to formally adopt Jenna?"

"Sure. If that's what Linda wants. As long as you guarantee that the kid keeps my name, anything is fine with me."

Why did this matter to Just? Justin wanted to ask, but he wasn't sure he'd like the answer. It had to be a selfish motivation, some idiotic idea about immortality through the offspring. Genes weren't enough for Just, he had to pass his name on as well. "Good." Justin stood up. He felt as if he couldn't bear to stay another second in the room. "Let's go, Laura."

"Not even a thank you?" Just asked, his face a mimicry of hurt. Justin opened his mouth, struggling with himself. In the end, he nodded politely to his father. "Thank you. The paperwork will be there for you to sign as soon as possible."

"You didn't tell me what you do for a living, son," Just asked. He stood up and walked them to the door, then stood with his hand on the doorknob, preventing them from leaving. "What line of business are you in?"

The calculating look tensing his father's features wasn't exactly a poker face. "I'm a teacher," Justin said tersely.

His father's hopeful look vanished. "A teacher. I see. University?"

"No. Ten-year-olds."

"Oh. No money in that, is there?"

"No." Justin turned to his father. "Since you're so well off now, I expect you will be sending child support for Jenna regularly?"

His father tore the door open and gestured for them to leave. "Sorry. If you're adopting the child, you're adopting the child, and you give up all claims to child support."

Justin took a deep breath as soon as they were out in the open again. "Thank God he agreed so easily. I don't know if I would've been able to go see him again. Now we just have to hope the adoption goes through before he realizes I'm not as broke as he thinks I am.''

"He didn't even ask any questions," Laura sputtered. "None. Not if you had a wife or children, if you had a house, if you could provide for the baby. Doesn't he care at all what happens to his daughter?"

"I told you what he was like," Justin said. "Her mother does care, at least. She may not be able to take care of her daughter, but she does love her."

"Maybe…" Laura stopped. "Never mind."

"What is it?"

"Well, I was just going to suggest you took Jenna to see her once in a while, but it's none of my business."

Justin nodded. "We'll have to talk about it. See what Linda wants, and what will be best for Jenna."

"That would be good," she agreed.

Justin was silent for a while. They walked back to Laura's car, and he strapped Jenna safely in the back. "Did you hear?" he asked as she pulled into the street. "The reason he didn't allow me to be adopted was so that I'd keep his name?"

"Yes. I heard."

Justin sighed, clenching and unclenching his fists. "It doesn't matter. If I'd been adopted, I might never have met Jenna. My sister wouldn't have anyone. It all turned out for the best in the end."

"Tomorrow you should start the process," Laura said. "Talk to Social Services, get a lawyer—I'm available if you like, but you might want to get a specialist in adoptions—try to get the adoption through as quickly as you can. Before Just decides he wants money for that signature. Everything will be easier when it's all settled."

Justin nodded. "For the moment, I'm just relieved this part is over."

There was silence as they drove through the city. Before returning home, they stopped at a fast-food restaurant for a late dinner, but it was silent as well. Laura didn't offer much conversation. It was obvious Justin needed solitude in his thoughts.

"Well," she said, as they approached his apartment door. "I'll see you after work tomorrow. Good luck. Call me if there's a problem."

Justin grabbed her hand, just as she was moving out of reach. "Aren't you forgetting something?"

Absolutely not. She hadn't forgotten that promised kiss. In fact, it had been occupying her thoughts most of the ride home. But she *had* thought he'd forgotten all about it. "Oh, you're right." She removed Pat's diaper bag from her shoulder and deposited it on his. "There you go. Good night."

"I don't think so."

She tried to look innocent when he pulled her to him again, but the grin gave her away. Justin frowned. "So you're teasing me, hmm? Pretending to have forgotten about our agreement?" He held on to her with one hand, the car seat with the other and stared helplessly at his front door. "You still have the key I gave you, don't you?"

"Yeah."

"Well, open the door, will you? My hands are busy."

"Afraid I'll run away?"

"Terrified."

She opened the door with her left hand, smiling as Justin dragged her inside. He pushed the door shut, put the car seat on the floor, and cornered her off against the wall. "That's better. I didn't want to put on a show in case any neighbors walked by."

Laura grinned. The baby was gurgling behind him, but other than that there was silence, only the sound of his breathing. He was close enough that she felt the movements of his chest with every breath. Warmth licked through her as their eyes met, and the heat in his gaze incinerated the grin right off of her face. She didn't realize she had whispered his name until he smiled and repeated her name back. She wasn't sure who'd moved first, but by that time it didn't matter, since the melting together was a mutual effort. His hair was soft under her fingers, his body hot as it pressed into hers, his mouth sweet and urgent, and somehow the universe was finally just as it should be.

Jenna interrupted, her soft gurgles changing into a whine that told them she would be wanting some attention very soon.

The kiss ended, but their embrace didn't. Not right away.

"Laura…" he whispered, his mouth at her ear, and his arms tightened around her. She turned her face into his neck, and felt at home. In fact she felt…in love.

Oh, Lord. Things were getting *way* out of hand.

"I…have to go…" she croaked, pushing him away with both hands. "Work tomorrow. Early. Need sleep." She grabbed for the doorknob and pulled the door open.

"Don't work too hard," he said as she left, leaving her brain behind, along with her heart, even forgetting to say goodbye to Jenna.

She was crawling into bed just as she heard the shower running on the other side of the wall. A few seconds later the rumble of Justin's singing drifted through the wall for the first time since he'd found out she'd been listening to his nightly concerts. She put a pillow over her face to suppress the giggles as she heard the silly improvised lyrics, clearly composed for her benefit.

Still grinning, she turned on her side when everything was silent again and snuggled into the pillow. Yeah, it sure sounded like their kiss had managed to cheer him up.

CHAPTER EIGHT

IT WAS barely noon, Monday morning, when Laura was interrupted by a human hurricane blasting into her office, slamming the door shut. Startled, she jumped to her feet, astonished to see Justin standing there, fists clenched on his hips and a dangerous fire in his eyes.

Something was very wrong.

"Justin?" She looked behind him, hoping to see Jenna there in her car seat or the stroller they'd borrowed from Steve, but there was no sign of the baby. "What's wrong? What are you doing here? Where's Jenna?"

Justin braced his fists on the wall for a few seconds, then hit it so hard that the result was a good imitation of a small earthquake.

"They took her, Laura." His voice was raw as he rested his head against the wall. "They took Jenna from me."

Laura's heart jumped and started racing. She shot across the room to Justin and grabbed his arm, forcing him to turn around and look at her. "What? Who? Who took Jenna?"

He didn't answer, so she grabbed his arm tighter and shook, almost shouting. "Tell me, Justin! What happened?"

"Social Services. I went to see them this morning, and they took her from me. She's been put in temporary foster care."

"Oh, Justin." Laura put her arms around him, even

though his pain and anger vibrated through the air and formed a formidable wall. He allowed her to hold him only for a second before pulling away to stand at the window, his body trembling with anger and energy that had no outlet.

"Justin, I'm so sorry."

Justin's arms were crossed, his hands clenched into fists. He was looking rather intimidating, and she wondered just how noisy his exchange with the social workers had been. Hopefully hadn't done anything to damage their case.

His case, she corrected herself.

She went into professional mode, and took his arm, motioning him to sit down, but he resisted. She sat down herself anyway, staring up at him. "Let's talk, Justin. Tell me everything. Did you bring a lawyer with you?" She sighed. "I shouldn't have let you go alone. I should have accompanied you. What was I thinking?"

He shook his head. "No lawyer. I didn't think I'd need one, at least so soon. They had me in there for almost two hours, asking all sorts of questions, and then sent me away alone." He cursed, twisting around again to stare out the window. "Stupid, going without a lawyer. Didn't I learn anything, growing up?"

"What did they say? What reason did they give you for taking her from you?"

Justin was shaking his head, as if to say he didn't want to talk at all.

"Justin, if you tell me everything I might be able to sort this out. I know the legal side of the system." She swore. "You're her brother. How could they do this?"

"They recognized me," he said suddenly.

"What do you mean?"

"I wasn't the perfect kid, Laura. I was the 'bane of their existence.'" He tapped his fingers rapidly on the window. His profile was hard, uncompromising. "My social worker loved that pun. And guess what? She's still working there. And she hasn't forgotten anything about the peanut butter I smeared on her car seat."

"Your old social worker's feelings about you shouldn't have anything to do with Jenna's case, let alone some silly pranks with peanut butter."

Justin shrugged, still vibrating with anger. "Tell it to them. They took my sister."

"Where is she? What did they say would happen?"

"They said they'd be putting her in temporary foster care until they'd reviewed the case," he recited in monotone. "And they wouldn't give me any idea about how long it would take."

"I should have expected this," Laura muttered. "I should have prepared you for this possibility. I'm sorry."

He twisted around to face her. "What do you mean, you should have expected this? You knew this would happen? You knew, and you let me take her to them?"

"Justin, there was no choice. If you hadn't, sooner or later they'd have come to take her away, and then you wouldn't have any chance of getting her back. You had to go to the authorities. But I should have realized that it wouldn't be that easy, even though you're her brother."

Justin started pacing the floor. "Explain this to me. What's the problem? What are my chances? What can I do to make sure I get her back?"

"The problem is that they aren't generally too eager to let single men have custody. Add to that Jenna's age.

There are many openings for the small ones, so many couples desperate for an infant, so she'd be easy to place with a suitable couple.''

"I'm her brother!" Justin banged on her desk with his fist to make his point. "Her *brother!* How can they place her with strangers when she already has family to take her in?"

Laura reached out and touched the back of his hand. "I'm on your side, remember?"

Justin stared at her for a minute. "Sorry."

She nodded. "You're a single man," she repeated. "The system is very family-orientated, with family being defined as a married couple, a father and a mother for the adopted child. But don't give up yet. There's always a chance. Your application is already in the system, and we should hear soon." She hesitated. "You didn't…make a scene, did you? Or tell them your feelings about Social Services?"

Justin said a word he probably wouldn't have used in front of Jenna. "Of course not. I knew I would damage my chances if I lost my temper. I was so polite and cooperative that my face almost bled from keeping up the smile. There's nothing there they can use against me."

"That's good. That's excellent."

"If the application is rejected, what happens then? Can I appeal? There must be something I can do."

"Of course there is. Relax, Justin. I know it's not fair, but losing your temper won't get us anywhere."

Justin finally dropped into a chair and rubbed over his face with his hands. "Okay. Calming down. We'll work through this."

"We will. I'll do everything I can to help. Don't lose hope yet."

He stared at the floor for a minute, then looked up and she was amazed to see him make an effort to smile at her. "What would I do without you?"

"Screw things up, probably."

"Yeah. Probably. I do appreciate everything you've been doing." He reached a hand toward her. "Come here."

She took his hand and let him pull her closer. "What?"

"I need distraction. Besides, I bet you've never been kissed at work."

Her insides quivered at the softness of his voice, especially when his arms came around her and she suddenly found herself sitting on his lap. "Well, I suppose it depends on your definition of a kiss. There was this episode during my internship, involving the senior Mr. Warren, a Christmas party and a bunch of mistletoe, but I think he mistook me for his personal assistant of forty years. He'd dropped his glasses into the punch bowl."

"I see. Did the earth move?"

"Yes. I backed into the water cooler and it tumbled over. The floor definitely moved."

"Want to see if we can top that experience?"

She wrapped her arms around his neck and bit his lower lip gently. He tasted wonderful. He smelled wonderful. And his eyes were still just as delicious as chocolate.

Oh, yes, she was in deep trouble.

"I have to confess I'm tempted. But what if my boss catches me making out in my office?"

"Tell him you're taken."

She was?

It sure felt like it, when a few seconds later his kiss made her forget that she was in her office, with her colleagues just one door away. There was an urgency in his touch that she understood, a need she felt compelled to fulfil. He needed her. And she needed him. It was undeniable.

No one interrupted them, but the sudden shrill of the phone ringing had her jumping out of his lap.

Just in time, she realized, seeing what she'd done to Justin's shirt. She refastened the top button of her own blouse and cleared her throat, appalled.

"We do pick the most appropriate time and places," Justin said with a crooked grin, reading her mind. Laura shook her head and pressed a button on the phone to divert the call to the switchboard. She didn't feel up to speaking to anyone for a minute or two.

Justin stood up. "I guess I'll go home. Are there any lawyers you'd recommend? Specialists in adoptions?"

"Sure. I'll jot down a few names."

She quickly made a small list and handed it to Justin, who thanked her with a kiss on the cheek and started opening the door.

Laura gasped and shot toward him, slamming the door shut before it had opened more than a few inches. "You can't walk through the building looking like this!" she whispered harshly. "I'd never live it down."

Justin looked confused, so she started buttoning his shirt and tucking it back into his jeans. She straightened his collar and stood on tiptoes to finger comb his hair.

"There," she said, looking him up and down. "You don't look anymore like you've spent the last few hours being ravished on my desk."

Justin laughed. He put his hand on her nape and gave her a kiss so sweet it almost brought tears to her eyes. "Thank you, Laura. Let's have dinner at my place tonight, okay? Just let yourself in with your key when you come home."

"Okay," she whispered as he opened the door. She watched him make his way to the elevator and vanish inside before closing the door and leaning against it with eyes shut.

Taken, was she?

Oh, yes. Her heart was definitely taken.

Going home from work was so much better, knowing someone was waiting. Getting up the steps was a breeze. She cautioned herself against getting too deep into romantic fantasies—there was Jenna to think about first—but after those kisses at the office, and after realizing he'd crept into her heart while she wasn't looking, it wasn't easy.

Justin was on-line, browsing through adoption regulations and court verdicts. She put her hand on his shoulder and squeezed gently. "Hi. How are you doing?"

Justin shrugged, but covered her hand with his for a moment. "Impatient. Worried. I phoned some of the lawyers you recommended, but didn't hire anyone yet. I guess I was afraid I'd hire the wrong person."

"Don't worry too much, Justin. We'll try to get through this all as quickly as we can." She wasn't as optimistic as she let on. Even if Justin eventually got custody of Jenna, even permission to adopt her, the process could take months. Even years. Far too long.

Justin stared up at the ceiling, brows heavy. "I've been thinking. This wouldn't be an issue at all if I were married, would it? As her brother, with a wife, I'd almost automatically get her?''

Laura pulled up a chair next to him and sat down. She nodded. ''It would be different. You could prove a stable home life, plus you're a blood relative.''

''Good.'' Justin leaned forward, resting his elbows by the keyboard and covering his face with his hands. ''Then that's what I'll do.''

''What?''

''I'll get married. If that's the only way to get Jenna back, I'll get married.''

She stared at him. ''Married?''

''Yes.''

''Are you serious?''

''Yes. If that's what it takes…''

Good thing she had sat down. He had to be kidding. Either that or he was delusional. She swallowed, wondering if her voice still worked. ''I see,'' she croaked. ''Got a wife lined up already?''

He turned to face her, his dark eyes troubled. ''Laura…I know you love her too. If we get married…''

Laura's heard started pounding until she heard nothing but the rush of blood in her ears. ''What are you trying to say?'' she managed to ask.

''I know it's a lot to ask. It would be just temporary. Just until everything is settled and we can be sure she won't be taken away.''

''Me?'' Her voice rose in hysteria. ''You want me to marry you?''

''Just for a few days.''

''Just for a few days?''

She'd always pictured a somewhat more romantic proposal from the man she loved.

"It'll just be a practical arrangement, of course."

"Of course," she repeated faintly. Practical. They had landed in this mess together, she'd insisted on helping him and Jenna through this, and she was *practical*.

What on earth had possessed her to get her head in the clouds over a few kisses?

"I wouldn't expect you to help me raise Jenna, of course," Justin continued. "In fact, it'd probably be better if you didn't have too much to do with her, so she wouldn't miss you too much when you're gone."

It was better that she didn't have much to do with Jenna? She pulled hard on her hair to keep herself from shouting. Amazingly her voice was calm. "Where am I going, Justin? I live next door."

"I guess we'll be moving. To a house. Jenna needs a yard to play in. Grass under her feet when she starts walking."

"Moving?"

"I mean, just me and Jenna," he hastened to explain. "When all this is over. I'm not expecting you to move with us. I'm already asking far too much of you. We would stay here until things are settled."

Just me and Jenna.

Of course.

She bit the inside of her cheek and tried to think rationally. Justin was focusing what was best for his little sister. He didn't have any idea how brutal his words felt. "It would be more than a few days," she said tonelessly. "The whole process could take up to a year."

"Are you saying no?"

She stood up and started pacing back and forth, fingers at her temples. She couldn't let him see her disappointment, or the stupid tears she was sure were gathering in her eyes. She blinked rapidly and worked hard at keeping her voice cool and distant. "Well, for one thing, Justin, I have to admit that this is not the proposal of my dreams."

"I know," he muttered. "You'd want a man you loved, down on one knee with a ring he'd sweated two years to buy and plans of together forever."

"Well, yeah, I'm afraid I do have the usual girlish fantasies. They're bred into us along with the ideal of Barbie's measurements. Mutual love, yes. Knee, a nice quaint touch. The expensive ring is optional, but the together forever part is not."

"Just forget it, Laura," he said tiredly. "I'll figure something out."

She stopped to glare at him, making a superhuman effort to disguise her feelings with humor. "Forget it? My first proposal? I don't think so."

It had the intended effect. Justin's face transformed in a surprised smile, then he laughed.

She turned to him, hands on hips and stomped on her feelings in order to get down to business. It wasn't hard to make up her mind. Jenna was too important. She'd gotten herself into this, she'd battle through. There'd be time enough later to lick her wounds. "Okay, let's specify this. How would it work? Would we live together?"

"I suppose we would have to, while the case is still being processed, yes. Until everything is settled."

She stared at him for a while, hand on her forehead, pushing her hair back. "Okay. I'll do it."

"You will?" Justin sat still, his eyes wide as he stared up at her. He wasn't looking very relieved. Actually, he was looking terrified. "Really? You will?"

She almost felt like denying it, just to wipe the panic

from his eyes. But this was what he wanted. What Jenna needed. They would have to set their own feelings aside, and think about the little girl they both loved. "Yes. I'll marry you. For Jenna," she emphasized. "I'm not doing you any favors, Justin, I'm doing this for your sister. If you haven't changed your mind by tomorrow. Getting married is no small thing."

"I won't change my mind. I'll do anything for Jenna. Anything."

Laura bit the inside of her cheek, pondering her new role as 'Anything'. She took deep breaths, trying to gain control of the sick horror that billowed inside as things became more and more real. She wasn't a part of this equation, she was just the hired help.

And the worst part was the controlled panic in his eyes. Even such a fake commitment to her seemed to be scaring the living daylights out of him.

She'd been so wrong to get her hopes up. He didn't share her feelings at all, did he? "Yeah. Anything. For Jenna. We'll get married for her."

"As soon as possible?"

She nodded. "Whenever. It only takes a day to get a license."

"Okay. Shall we say Friday, then?"

"Friday?"

"Yeah. There will be a meeting at Social Services a week from now, so I want us to be married by the end of the week. Would that be okay with you?"

Laura gulped down air. Married woman by Friday, would that be okay with her?

"No problem."

No problem.

Hah!

Could life get any more complicated that this?

Laura sat in her car outside her parents' home, post-poning the inevitable.

The marriage license had been sitting in her purse since this morning. That part had been easy—all they had to do was show up with their IDs. The tricky part would be explaining to her parents how this worked.

It wouldn't really be hard to explain to her parents that by the weekend, she'd be a married woman with a stepdaughter. They'd embrace Justin and Jenna—they already had. But explaining to them that this was strictly a marriage of convenience, something from out of the Middle Ages—that was a toughie.

Add to that her own raw and bruised feelings, and it was pretty obvious that this wasn't going to be fun.

Her mother finally appeared in one of the windows, peering out, and then smiling and waving as she noticed her daughter. Laura waved back and took several deep breaths, bracing herself for the ordeal ahead. She undid her seatbelt slowly, and opened the door, just as slowly.

Beth had opened the front door to welcome her, be-fore she was even halfway up the path. "Laura! How nice to see you." She put her arms around Laura and squeezed her. "And happy birthday again, darling."

Right. It was her birthday. That fact hadn't even crossed her mind yet.

"Three times in one week that I get to see you. This has to be a record. Did your boss finally decide you were worth more alive than dead?"

Laura smiled and hugged her mother back. "Some-thing like that. Hi Mom. Is Dad home?"

"No, he's at the hardware store. Should be back in time for dinner." Beth shook her head as she put her arms around Laura's shoulder and pulled her inside. "Apparently none of the six million nails in the garage is exactly the right one to use to hang our new painting."

"I see. Well. Good. Actually, it's better it's just you right now, anyway." It might be more difficult for her father to accept his daughter entering a fake marriage. Better that Mom find out first. Wasn't it?

"Why? Is there something wrong?"

Laura rubbed her hands together, aimlessly wandering into the kitchen, back out, through the living room and then toward her old bedroom, which was now the guest-room and home office. Her mother followed, a frown of worry and concern growing deeper with every moment.

"What's wrong, darling?"

"Nothing." Laura sat down on her old bed, fiddling with the bedspread. "Nothing's wrong. But I have some-thing to tell you." She took a deep breath and motioned for her mother to sit next to her. "Mom, I want you to listen until I'm finished, and don't jump to conclusions, okay?"

"Okay." Beth got comfortable, and took a deep breath. She grabbed Laura's hand in hers. "This sounds serious, darling. Are you pregnant?"

Laura groaned. "No."

"What is it, then?"

Laura sighed. "Listen… It's about Justin. And about Jenna."

Her mother nodded.

"Social Services took Jenna away from him. He's fighting for custody now. His chances will improve a lot if he gets married."

"I see…" her mother replied with caution, seeming

not ready to make the obvious jump in conclusion. Laura gulped down some air and braced herself.

"So, Mom, I'm going to help him."

"I see. How?"

"I'm going to marry him."

Beth squealed and hugged her. "I was hoping you'd say that! You're getting married! That's wonderful, darling! I knew it the moment I saw him. I told your father: 'That's the man for Laura.' Wait, let me get pen and paper. We need to make plans. You need to get married soon, because of the baby, don't you? That's okay, we'll just scale our plans down a bit. It'll be a wonderful wedding anyway. Let's see, where did I put my notepad?"

Oh, God. Runaway train already. Her mother was rummaging in a drawer, humming with pleasure. Laura stood up, and tugged on her mother's arm to get her to sit down and pay attention. "Mother, listen! This isn't a real marriage. It's a marriage in name only, just so that Justin gets the baby. Not a real marriage."

Her mother gave her a look of disbelief. "You'll be legally married?"

"Yes."

"And you'll be living together?"

"Yes."

"And you're in love with him?"

"Yes…I mean, no!"

A unique Mom-grin. "Gotcha."

"Mom!" Laura whined, feeling twelve years old. "You tricked me."

"Have you told him?"

"Of course not."

"What about him?"

"He's not in love, if that's what you're asking."

Her mother waved a hand, dismissing that small inconvenience. "I wouldn't be too sure. I saw the way he looked at you. When's the wedding?"

Laura sighed in relief that her mother wasn't prying further. She was pretty proud at the control she had over her emotions now, but it wouldn't take much to crumble her defenses. "We got the license this morning. We're getting married on Friday."

Beth's brow crinkled. "Let's say Saturday. Friday is too busy, on top of the short notice."

"We don't need notice, Mom. We're going to city hall, just the two of us."

"Nonsense." Beth jumped to her feet, responding to some sound Laura didn't hear. "Your father is back. Let's go tell him!"

"Oh, my God," Laura whimpered, almost crawling into Justin's apartment.

Justin grinned, watching her settle in his sofa and grab a blanket to wrap around herself. "You look like you could use some ice cream, birthday girl."

"Yes. Lots and lots of it. Got chocolate syrup?"

"Yup." Justin vanished into the kitchen, appearing a few minutes later with a big bowl of ice cream. Laura eyed it with a mixture of greed and apprehension, not unlike the way she tended to eye the man holding the bowl, she thought cynically. Neither of them was particularly good for her health.

"Justin, you're the worst thing that has ever happened to my waistline, you know." As well as to her heart.

"I'm trying to get you from scrawny to skinny. Stop complaining." He knelt beside her, and spoon-fed her ice cream. "What happened? A bad day at work?"

"No. Worse."

"Spill."

"I told my parents. About us getting married." The ice cream was yummy. So was getting fed. It was deliciously decadent to just lie there and let Justin feed her.

"I see. How bad was it?"

"Bad." She whimpered, and opened her mouth wide for a new spoonful of ice cream.

"I see. Am I scheduled for a lynching?"

"No. That's the problem. They're ecstatic. They refuse to listen. They think we're marrying for *love*." Somehow she managed to make the word sound sarcastic.

"Didn't you tell them about Jenna and the custody problem?"

She was too tired to shrug. "Yes. Not that it did me much good. You've met my mother. You know what's she's like. Selective hearing. One-way street. She wants me married, and she's already cleared a spot on the mantelpiece for our wedding picture. More ice cream, please? It's melting."

Justin resumed his slave-duties. "She wants you married, even to someone like me?"

She opened one eye. "What's wrong with someone like you?"

"Well, I don't think I could be considered the model son-in-law material."

"Hah! If you pass my mother's muster, you pass anyone's. And she adores you. It's the baby thing. She's one of those women who can't resist a man with a baby on his shoulder." The weakness must be genetic. Her mother probably also had a soft spot for Eau De Baby

Vomit. No wonder she'd managed to fall for Justin. It was her genes' fault.

Justin put the empty bowl on the table and sat down opposite her. "I'm sorry. Do you want me to talk to them?"

Laura raised her head and looked at Justin, picturing him in her parents' living room, explaining earnestly to them, that no, he didn't love Laura, she was just doing him a favor, and he was very grateful. She could picture her father looking at her mother, asking: "Didn't you say she was in love with this guy?"

Confiding in mothers was never a good idea.

"No," she sighed. "I don't think that'll do much good."

"Anything I can do?"

There were shadows under his eyes, and he was looking more tired after a single night without Jenna than after all the sleepless nights before. The separation from his sister was hard on him, and she felt an acute longing to make things right. She raised a hand to his cheek. "Yes."

"What?"

The temptation to ask for a kiss was killing her. Especially with the slight abrasiveness of his jaw against her palm, and his dark eyes so solemn and questioning. She could almost feel his lips against hers, warming them after the coldness of the ice cream. She could almost feel his hair under her fingers, his breath on her face.

"Laura?" It was a whisper, tempting her further as his eyes darkened even more and she read an answering desire in his eyes. "What are you thinking?"

God, how she wanted to kiss him. The need was almost painfully intense. She had fallen in love with him, and if she kept this up, he'd find out. She'd blurt it out, or reveal it in her kisses. He'd find out.

That couldn't happen. Not now. Not when there was so much riding on them getting through this marriage without any complications. Like escaping with her heart and sanity more or less intact. The only way to do that was to keep distant. And this wasn't just about her and Justin anymore. There was an innocent child involved. She couldn't let her emotions cause trouble for little Jenna. For so many reasons, emotional distance from Justin was now more important than ever.

She broke eye contact and reached for the bowl, pushing it into his chest. He looked down, puzzled. "Ice cream," she said loudly. "I was thinking about ice cream. Can I have some more?"

Justin fetched her more ice cream, feeling slightly disoriented. He'd been sure she wanted him to kiss her, but then she'd rammed the bowl into his chest hard enough to bruise, and told him all she wanted was more ice cream. He shook his head as he absently piled the bowl full. He was getting married. He was getting married to Laura, and he hadn't even made it into her shower yet to experiment with washcloths and conditioner.

For Jenna, he reminded himself. They were doing this for Jenna. Both of them. Laura didn't like it any more than he did. And he didn't like it at all…did he? He took the bowl back into the living room where Laura was sitting, staring at the television tuned to a nature show, her expression telling him she wasn't seeing so much as one tentacle.

She was beautiful, he thought as he sat down next to

her and put the bowl on the coffee table in front of her. And in a few days, she'd be his wife. They'd be legally allowed to kiss and cuddle and have all the shower fun they wanted.

If they wanted.

He sighed so loudly that it broke Laura's spaced out concentration. "What?" she asked.

"Nothing. Just thinking about the marriage."

Laura nodded. "I know. Weird, isn't it?"

Her lips were so tempting. Watching her eat ice cream nearly killed him every single time. He leaned forward and cupped her jaw in his hand, warming her cold lips and tasting the sweet chocolate of the ice cream. She went still in surprise, but then she responded and he shuddered in a mixture of relief and longing when her arms came around his neck. Sweet. Cold lips gradually turning warm, colder tongue that needed the warmth of his. Her heartbeat against his fingers at the side of her neck, her warm shoulder in his palm. Warmth… Heat… Sizzle…

Cold!

Justin yelped and jumped to his feet.

"I'm sorry!" Laura's voice was shocked. "I didn't mean to…I wasn't watching the ice cream." She grabbed the paper towel he'd brought her with the ice cream and reached out. "Let me…"

"No!" he bit out, snatching the paper towel out of her hand. "Not a good idea."

"I'm sorry…" she repeated, but this time she was fighting a smile.

"Don't worry," Justin muttered, heading toward his bedroom to change clothes. "It was time for a cold shower anyway."

Not that it had worked. A whole bowl of ice cream dumped on him, and most of all he'd wanted to ignore it and continue what they'd been doing.

But it wasn't smart. It wasn't fair. She was helping him out, sacrificing a lot for him and his baby sister—the last thing she deserved was for him to mess up her life even more. Sure, there were a lot of sparks between them, but she'd made it clear she was marrying him for Jenna—only for Jenna. He had to remember that, despite the force of his feelings for Laura, despite the rising conviction—terrifying, but true—that if she felt the same way, he would be prepared to take risks he'd never even contemplated taking before.

He cursed under his breath as he ripped a clean T-shirt out of his closet with unnecessary force. His feelings were irrelevant. He was in her debt, and he owed it to her to make this whole thing as uncomplicated and painless as possible.

It wasn't going well so far. Getting involved was not the way to make things painless. Kissing her was not the way to make things uncomplicated. For either of them.

He rested his head against the wooden door of the closet and closed his eyes for a moment. Laura was marrying him—and that meant he couldn't kiss her anymore.

For a simple solution, this was sure turning out to be a convoluted one.

There was no escaping Laura's parents. Laura wasn't sure how that had happened, despite her intentions of staying away from her folks until the marriage was a signed and sealed fact, but Wednesday evening she found herself on her parents' doorstep, with a rather uncomfortable Justin at her side.

"You've nothing to worry about," she whispered to him once more, taking his hand and squeezing it. "I told you, they're thrilled about this wedding, and they're not listening to anything about it not being a real one. Don't worry, and don't bother trying to convince them. I already did. It won't work. They think we're in love, and that the situation with Jenna is simply speeding things up a bit."

Justin shifted his weight and cast a glance backward as if contemplating an escape. "That doesn't exactly reassure me, Laura," he grumbled. "It probably means your father is coming after me with a shotgun and a hand-carved tombstone when we divorce."

Could you stop talking about that divorce, Laura almost yelled at him. It wasn't something she wanted to think about. It was something she dreaded more than she dreaded standing by Justin's side on Friday, promising to love and honor him forever.

Because she already did.

Her head was spinning again as the door opened and her father appeared, hugging both of them with enthusiasm. Her mother came running from the kitchen, preceded by heavenly aromas, and wrapped one arm around each of them. "Wonderful to see you! You know, you look great together. Like you match each other. We're all so excited."

"All?"

Laura heard Justin whimper at her side as they were pulled into the living room to face her brothers and their entire families. His hand tightened around hers and she heard him take a deep breath.

Steve and Roy were both sizing Justin up, looking far less excited than her parents.

"Marriage of convenience, huh?" Roy asked, his eyes on Justin only. "What's that all about?"

Beth shushed him. "The baby is speeding things up a bit, that's all. She's not the first baby to get a wedding date on the table." She turned to Justin. "How's the little one?" she asked. "Is she okay?"

Justin nodded. "Laura assures me she's okay, with good people. I trust her. Otherwise I and Jenna would be fugitives by now."

Laura knew he was only half joking. "I pulled some strings and managed to find out who the temporary foster family is," she told them. "I'm sure they are trustworthy. There's no need to worry, she's in more capable hands than she was with us."

Her mother frowned. "Who could be more capable than you two? But I'm glad they're good people." She took their hands in each of hers and dragged them away again, down the hall and into the guestroom. "I've been on the computer all day, surfing wedding sites. I've found so many fun things I want to show you. Even on such short notice, there's no reason not to make this a memorable wedding."

"Mom!" Laura sent Justin an apologetic look. "I told you—this isn't a real wedding. It's not a real marriage. We're just doing this for Jenna's sake."

"Then for Jenna's sake, look at this website here. You want her to look at her parents' wedding pictures and sigh over how beautiful her mother was. What about this one?"

"I won't be Jenna's mother."

"See the veil that comes with this one? How lovely.

Then of course there's my old wedding gown, if you want to try it on. I already called Reverend Mitchell, he was thrilled to hear the news. Saturday at two. He booked the church, and I've ordered the flowers, and invited people. Just the closest relatives.'' She grabbed a stack of open envelopes from the desk and handed them to Justin. ''Here are invitations for your side of the family. You just fill in the names, but you'll either have to give them in person or call them, the mail won't get there in time.''

''Mom!'' Laura was speechless over her mother's interference. ''I can't believe this...''

Beth patted her arm. ''I know you had just planned on a simple ceremony at city hall because of the time constraints and the circumstances. But I've got plenty of time. You just concentrate on your fiancé and the baby and your work, and I'll plan the wedding. You'll thank me later.''

''I can't...''

''If you're likely to get in trouble with Social Services, a real wedding is a lot more convincing,'' her mother pointed out. ''There's nothing like a white church wedding to prove that a couple is truly in love.''

''But...''

Justin's arm came over her shoulder. ''Laura...if this is true, there's no harm in having a slightly more elaborate wedding, is there?''

''Slightly more elaborate? Justin, are you nuts? This isn't a real marriage, why should be have a real wedding? Signing the damn documents is the only thing needed.''

His arm fell away, and she realized she had shaken it off. ''Of course. You're right.''

Laura stared at him for long moments, then grabbed his arm. "Mom, could you excuse us for just a minute? I need to talk to...my fiancé."

Beth nodded, and she dragged Justin out into the hall and locked the two of them in the bathroom. She leaned back against the shower cubicle and tried to gather her thoughts. "Justin, don't you mind?"

"Mind what?"

"All this! Don't you want to save a real wedding with all the trimmings for when you're getting married for real, to someone you love and want to spend the rest of your life with?"

Justin had been shaking his head all through her monologue. "It's not an issue for me. I won't be getting married again, and if a church wedding is something that will help my case, I'm all for it." He touched her cheek. "But I understand how you feel, wanting to save your real wedding for a real marriage." He squeezed her shoulder. "Tell you what—I'll talk to your parents and see if I can convince them."

"No!" She sighed. They were right. If the nature of their marriage was questioned and investigated, having the proof of a real church wedding could help their cause. This was for the best. If she was getting married for Jenna, turning her whole life upside down for the next year, wearing a real wedding gown shouldn't be that much of an additional sacrifice. "It'll be fine. If you're okay with it, I'm okay."

"You're sure?"

No.

"Yes."

Her mother had more ulterior motives for the visit. Of course she did. After dinner, Laura found herself standing in her parents' bedroom, wearing a thirty-five-year-old wedding gown that made her feel like a princess for a few precious seconds. Until she remembered the reality of what was happening.

Then she started crying.

"Honey...oh, no. Wait." Beth hurried to unbutton the dress. "I think it's lovely on you. What do you think? Do you prefer to rent or buy a dress?"

"N-o," Laura hiccupped, and Beth caught her tears with a tissue. "I lo-ove it. I real-really do."

"Darling, try to hold back those tears until I have the dress off. We can't have stains on it. Oh, Lord, how am I going to get you out of it?"

Laura grabbed her mother's terry robe off the bed and wrapped the arms around her neck, creating a giant bib. "There. Your robe can take tear stains, can't it?"

"Absolutely."

"Aren't you even going to ask what's wrong?"

"I don't need to. I know what's wrong."

"You do?" Laura hiccupped. "I'm not sure I do."

"Yes, you do. You've in love, and you're getting married, and you're not sure how your husband-to-be feels. You need to talk to him."

"I see. I'm supposed to ask him if he loves me?"

"Yes." Beth's eyes twinkled. "In a subtle way, of course."

"Oh." Laura digested that. "You mean something like running into a burning building and see if he rescues me?"

"Not in that dress, you won't."

Her giggles shook a few tears on to the robe. "Mom, I always knew you loved me."

Beth hugged her gingerly, careful not to crumple the

dress. "Talk to the man, Laura. I'm not having you get married in my dress if you aren't sure that's what you want. Talk to him."

Talk to him. Right.

She nodded to her mother. She'd talk to Justin. Tomorrow after work. She needed to clear one thing with her boss, then she'd have a serious talk with Justin.

If she was going to do this, she might as well go the whole nine yards. If she was going to be a mother to Jenna—even if just for a year—she might as well do it right.

CHAPTER NINE

"I WAS wondering if we could talk."

Justin looked up from his laptop, eyes cloudy with concentration. "Talk?" His eyes cleared as he saw the look on her face. He straightened up and closed the laptop. "Sure. Let's talk. What's on your mind?"

She opened her mouth to ask something subtle and intelligent, but blurted it out instead. "What kind of marriage is this going to be, Justin?"

"What do you mean?"

"For starters, where are we going to live? Here? In our two apartments?"

Justin glanced out the darkened window, a frown creasing his brow. "I haven't really thought far beyond getting Jenna back. I want to buy a house for us to live in. But I told you—I understand if you don't want to leave. I could wait with the move until we…well, until after the divorce."

Hysteria time. They weren't married yet, and he kept bringing up the divorce. What was she doing? Why did she insist on fantasizing about a future with this man, with this family? He didn't want a future with her, he just wanted a fake wife for a few months. After that, they'd divorce, he'd move away with Jenna and she'd probably never see them again.

"Laura? What's wrong? Do you want to back out?"

"No. No, I'm not backing out. I said I'd do this, and I will."

His eyes were watchful. "You look and sound like a brave human sacrifice. I don't want you to do this if that's how you feel."

"I'll be fine. I'm just having pre-wedding jitters."

"I don't blame you."

"Okay, more questions: what about my job?"

"What about it?"

"Are you expecting me to quit so I can take care of Jenna?"

Justin stared at her for a while, then looked up at the ceiling in frustration. "Laura, are you crazy? You're doing me the favor of getting married to me so I can get my sister back, and you think I'm expecting you to leave your job and become my kitchen slave?"

"Sorry. I just need to make sure."

"Why is your job so important to you, Laura? I mean, I understand ambition, but you seem to take it to extremes."

"It's important to me to get settled. To earn money."

"Money is important to you?"

"Of course. We didn't have lot of it. I was the youngest, and they wanted the best for me. My parents couldn't afford to send me to college, so my brothers helped. All of them sacrificed a lot for my education. I can never repay them for many years of going without, but maybe I can make up for it in a small way."

"Do you really think they expect payment?"

"No. But being a success, being good at what I do, and getting good compensation is the only way I can show them their efforts were worthwhile. Don't you understand?"

He nodded. "I understand."

"Anyway, I talked to my boss today." She took a

deep breath, praying he would understand—and yet that he wouldn't. She wasn't sure anymore if this had been a good idea. Not with the way things were. Justin might not approve. "Starting next month, I'm going down to half-time, at least for a year."

"Excuse me?" Justin said weakly, after a long silence. "You're doing what?"

"Going down to half time," she repeated. "I've already cleared it with my boss. I'll be home at noon. So I can look after Jenna in the afternoons, and you in the mornings. She'll always have one of us."

"You don't have to do that, Laura. You don't have to sacrifice your career."

She held up a hand to stop him. "I'm not sacrificing anything. I want to stay at home with her. I love her, and she needs me. It's worth it. I can afford working half-time for a year. I've made up my mind."

"But what happens when…" Justin rubbed his face and looked out the window again. "Aw, hell, Laura, I can't let you do this."

Her heart sank. The divorce. The inevitable divorce. Always at the forefront of his mind.

"Well, it's better to have loved and lost, isn't it?" she quipped.

Justin's head snapped back. "What do you mean?"

"Jenna. Weren't you worried about her feelings when we…when I…after I'm gone?"

"Yes. That, too. Of course."

"I won't just abandon her, Justin. That's a promise. We'll ease me out of the house. Maybe I could baby-sit her on weekends sometimes. We'll work it out."

"Are you sure you want to do this?"

She nodded. There wasn't any doubt anymore, hadn't

been since she'd decided to walk into her boss's office and discuss the possibility of changing her schedule. She hadn't expected a child to come along and change the way she felt about everything—but Jenna had. Jenna and Justin. She'd fallen in love with them both. It was a mess, but she knew what she had to do. For their sakes.

There was only one more question that needed to be asked.

"Just one more thing, Justin…I have to ask what you're thinking…I mean, will we have separate bedrooms?"

Justin's mouth fell open, and as he started to speak, she heard him stutter. He paused, and swore. "I haven't stuttered since I was ten years old."

Laura felt foolish. Of course he hadn't been expecting them to sleep together. Why should he? This was just a convenient arrangement. He'd been talking about a divorce just a minute ago. So what if they'd kissed a few times in a way that sent fiery flashes all the way to the bottom of her soul? It didn't mean they would have a real wedding night to celebrate their fake marriage.

"You're asking me if we're…" He broke off and rubbed his forehead with the back of his hand. "Sorry, would you rephrase the question? I'm not sure I understand."

Well, at least he hadn't said "no, thank you."

But she would not repeat the question. No way. She shook her head. "Forget it. It was another stupid question. This whole wedding business isn't good for my brain."

Justin looked out the window, and bit his lip. He shrugged. "Well, at least it has given you some very strange ideas about what I expect of you. I didn't expect you to quit work, and I didn't have any plans to demand my conjugal rights on our wedding night."

"Why not?"

Oh, God. She hadn't really asked that, had she?

Justin stared at her. "What? You think we should…"

"Forget it."

He grabbed her arm as she tried to pass him and leave the room. "No way." He dragged her toward him.

She rested her head against his shoulder, feeling stupid. "Sorry. I'm just confused. Not sure where all this is going. I'm letting my mother and her romantic wedding plans mess with my head. I always did expect to spend my wedding night in my husband's bed. What with the wedding dress and everything, I'm just going out of my mind…"

She would have rambled on a whole lot longer if she hadn't suddenly found herself on the sofa, being kissed so thoroughly that there was severe danger of anoxia. She didn't mind. Oxygen was an overrated substance.

She fiddled with the collar of his shirt, when she was finally free and had inhaled some emergency rations of air. All of a sudden she was floating with happiness, instead of being dragged down by confused despair. Maybe it wasn't rational, considering the circumstances, but there had been such emotion in his kiss, such promise, even if they were not pledges he felt he could make out loud. "You know, Justin, that's the kind of stuff married people do. What they do in their shared bedroom. That's why I was asking."

"Right. So it doesn't have anything to do with if we're married or not." He stroked her cheek with a finger. "How about this: We'll just pretend we're not married, and we'll be fine."

"Pretend we're not married?"

"Why not? Marrying for Jenna's sake just complicates things between us. We were doing great as it was. Let's not let one little marriage interfere with that."

Laura had to laugh, even though her head was spinning. Pretending not to be married? Interesting notion. "I think you're the most confusing man on the planet."

Justin's chuckle reverberated through her head as it rested on his shoulder. "Thank you."

Laura smiled. She felt safe now. He was right. Best thing was to get the wedding over with, and then carry on, pretending they weren't married at all. No. Just two people, caring for a small child together.

Maybe falling in love along the way. She already had, and Justin's touch said a lot about his own feelings. She shouldn't worry too much about setting her hopes too high. Things could work out.

Justin's heartbeat was strong under her palm. His breath hot in her hair. His hand was rubbing up and down her back, and everything seemed fine. Saturday they'd get married, and she didn't even have to lie at the altar. She did love him.

And he just might be starting to love her back. His brain might not want that to happen, not now, but his heart, pushing against her palm with every beat, was a different story.

It was healing.

CHAPTER TEN

LAURA had Friday afternoon off to prepare for the wedding, and found herself sitting in Justin's kitchen at lunch, eating a grilled cheese sandwich with ham, cheese, and something green that was probably good for her.

"So," she asked between bites. "What is all this 'preparing' we need to do? Hasn't Mom done just about everything?"

Justin shrugged. "Sounds like it. Maybe you should call her and see if there's anything we need to do."

The telephone rang, and Justin jumped to his feet, swearing as he searched for the cordless phone. He answered it tersely and spoke a few words. Laura kept eating her sandwich, amazed to find her nerves were still calm, only twenty-four hours away from the wedding. Justin's pretend-not-to-be-married idea seemed to be working.

Justin ended the phone call and she turned to him. "Justin, I've been thinking. I really wouldn't mind moving to a house with you and Jenna. I'm just renting this place, anyway. A move would be fine with me."

He didn't answer.

"Justin?"

He was standing, telephone in his hand at his side, and didn't seem to hear her.

"Justin? What's wrong?"

He didn't answer, just stared at her, face frozen, and

Laura's heart started racing. "What's wrong, Justin?" She stood up, grabbed the front of his shirt and shook him. "Justin! Tell me what's wrong! What is it? It's Jenna, isn't it? Something's happened to Jenna?"

"I'm sorry," Justin said faintly, covering her fists with a hand. "Jenna is fine, don't worry. I'm just so surprised." He swallowed, and finally put the phone away. "It was the social worker. My old social worker." At last, a smile spread over his face, relieving her anxiety. "I'm getting Jenna. The official paperwork is yet to be done, but they say that as her brother, after being interviewed the other day, and with the recommendation of both parents, I will have no problem with being granted full custody and a subsequent adoption."

Joy and relief ripped through her, giving her goose bumps. "Justin, that's wonderful." She hugged him tightly. "Can you believe it? Oh, God, I'm so relieved."

Justin was smiling broadly. It was something she hadn't seen in a while, and it warmed every inch of her. "She's coming home tomorrow morning."

Tomorrow. Laura crashed back to earth, the shock so great that she sagged against Justin, her legs barely holding her up. She'd almost opened her mouth to say how wonderful it was that Jenna could be present at their wedding.

There was no need for a wedding anymore.

Justin suddenly gave a loud whoop of joy. He grabbed her in a bear hug, and swirled her around the room before kissing her soundly. "I don't believe it. We don't have to get married. I'm getting Jenna!"

"Yes," she said, smiling, while trying to hide her eyes. If he looked too close, he would see those emerging tears of hurt and disappointment that she had no right to feel. "You're getting Jenna. It's wonderful."

Justin let go of her, a frown rising between his eyes. "*I'm* getting Jenna," he repeated.

"Yes. Congratulations, Justin. I know you'll take such good care of her."

Justin let go of her, and she stepped back. That was it. She was out of the picture. No longer was there any need to turn her life upside down so Jenna could have a home with her brother.

She should be happy. Not only for Justin and Jenna, but for herself.

"We don't have to get married," Justin said again, as if trying to convince himself he was really off the hook.

"No." She tried to add something, a cheerful comment on how wonderfully things were turning out, but nothing emerged. He could take that as he wanted, she couldn't summon up the will to keep up the pretense.

She looked around Justin's apartment, in a daze. So much of her stuff was here. Her own apartment had more or less gathered dust all week.

It was time to go home.

She managed to smile at Justin, who was looking at her, the look on his face suggesting he was battling a particularly tricky calculus problem. "I guess I should be going," she told him. "Mom needs to know about the change in plans. I'll take some of my stuff with me. I've been cluttering up your apartment."

Justin didn't answer, and his nod was almost nonexistent. She walked around the room, gathering up the stray things that somehow had migrated over here in the past weeks. A pen here, a plate from her kitchen there.

She even had a toothbrush and some other supplies in his bathroom, she remembered with a sigh.

Justin just watched her, arms crossed and that frown firmly in place, but he still didn't speak. She finally looked at him when she had all her stuff jammed in a couple of plastic bags. "That's all," she said. "Amazing how much junk I've brought over, isn't it?"

Justin's frown cut even deeper into his forehead. What was he thinking? Instead of asking, she inched toward the door, where she almost fell over the shopping bag she'd brought over yesterday.

Her wedding present to Justin. Just the thing she didn't want to look at right now.

"I have to go now," she said, scooping up the small bag and putting it in the pile with the rest of her bags. "I have to call my mother and make sure all the plans are canceled. It's very short notice. We have a lot of calls to make."

"Laura..." He stepped toward her, reached out, but didn't quite touch her. "Do we have to cancel everything?"

Laura's heart stopped for a second. "What do you mean?" she managed to ask.

He shrugged, looking uncomfortable. "I don't know...it's all been planned. I sort of got used to the idea. I just thought...maybe we should get married anyway..."

Laura whimpered. This hurt even more than the first proposal. Was he worried, now, about his ability to raise the child alone? Did he want her help? Or did he want to secure himself, just in case there would be trouble with the authorities again? "Why?" she choked out. "In case you have trouble with Social Services anyway?"

"No…"

"Because Jenna needs a mother?"

"No. Because I need you."

Laura shook her head, feeling weary with sadness. "No, you don't need me, Justin," she said. "You may think that now, because we've been in this together, but you don't. You'll learn how to be a single father. It'll be tough, but you'll adapt. And then maybe someday you'll find a woman you'll love and who loves you, and you'll want to get married for real, not just for convenience."

As speeches went, she was rather proud of that one. None of the tears threatening to reveal her feelings to him had leaked into her voice. Why was she being so miserable, anyway? It wasn't as if she was losing anything. She'd never had him. And it wasn't as if he were about to take his sister and walk straight out of her life. They'd stay in touch. Maybe. For a while, at least.

She turned away and gathered her bags together. The small shopping bag made her hesitate, wondering if to give it to him anyway. She'd chosen it for him, spending an inordinate amount of time on the task. The wedding was off, so maybe the gift was no longer appropriate. Then again, it was more appropriate than ever. Justin was embarking on a journey of fatherhood, alone. She stomped on the doubts and handed him the small bag. "Here. I bought you this."

Justin didn't take it. He just stared as if he'd never received a present before in his life. "What is it?"

"What does it look like? It's a present."

"A present? For me? Why?"

Laura shrugged. "It was supposed to be my wedding

gift to you. Since there won't be a wedding, you might as well get it now.''

Justin kept staring at her, not moving to take the package.

"My arm is getting tired, Justin. Would you please just take it? I wanted to give you this, okay? Don't make a big deal out of it.''

Justin finally reached for the package, just as she was beginning to wonder if it would have been a better idea to jam it in one of the plastic bags with her other stuff. This had seemed the perfect gift at the time. She wasn't sure anymore. Maybe it was just stupid. She bit her lip and waited for him to open it.

Justin turned the package slowly over in his hands before starting to remove the paper. Carefully. Slowly peeling off each bit of tape. But finally, the wrappings were off and he held the contents, looking astonished.

"Well?" The silence had dragged on too long for her piece of mind. Could she have offended him? Did he think it was ridiculous? "What do you think?''

He didn't answer, and she squirmed uncomfortably. What was wrong? "Justin, it's just a teddy bear, not a machine gun.''

Justin was holding the bear with both hands, his face astonished when he finally dragged his gaze from the bear to look at her. "You bought me a teddy bear. My first teddy bear.'' The smile was faint, but warm. "You remembered, didn't you?'' he whispered. "What I said about never having had one?'' He traced the bear's head with his fingers, stroking the soft ears. "I don't believe you did this.''

She shrugged, still feeling defensive. "I saw him. He reminded me of you. Cuddly, yet scowling a bit. I thought you'd need him now. But you can always give it to Jenna."

Justin slid his hand into her hair and had pulled her closer for a kiss that was over before she realized it had begun. "No. Jenna has her own teddy bears. This one is mine." He kissed her again. "Thank you."

"You're welcome."

There were emotions in his eyes that she could only define as joy and relief. Freedom, almost, a sense of wonder.

All that because of one teddy bear?

He rubbed his nose against hers. "So you think I'm cuddly, huh?"

A smile hovered on her lips as an answering sense of wonder began to bloom inside her. "In a macho motor-cyclical way, of course."

"Of course."

Third kiss in the space of a minute. The teddy bear was now sitting on the table beside them, as Justin's hands cradled her neck, and then moved up into her hair, warm and steady. "Thank you," he repeated against her lips, his words barely a whisper. "And I hope you don't mind my kissing you. It's the teddy bear's fault. If I stop kissing you, I'm liable to start crying like a baby instead, and I wouldn't want to do that. It's not macho."

"I'm fine with the kissing," she murmured back, her own arms around his neck. "I wouldn't want you to lose that macho image. Next thing, you'd be selling the bike."

"No way. What do you think I got you that helmet for? I may have to trade it in for a station wagon for Jenna's sake, but I'm not selling the bike until you agree to take a ride with me."

His kisses were quite intoxicating. Brief, but warm and loving, and the way he had his hands in her hair and one of his legs wrapped around hers to hold her close made her feel like the only object in his universe. Nothing seemed impossible now—not even surviving a motorcycle ride.

"I might be persuaded," she conceded. "If you promise you'll be careful."

"I'm always careful. I wouldn't let anything happen to you."

"I know."

The kissing thing was getting out of hand, she thought vaguely a few minutes later, quite happy with that general idea. Out of hand was exactly where she wanted it to get. She smiled against Justin's mouth and burrowed even closer to him.

But then he was suddenly five inches away and smiling, instead of panting with lust like he was supposed to. He took her hand before she could pull him back. "Great. Let's go."

"What? Where?" Completely disoriented, she let him drag her out of the apartment and down the stairs. For a long moment there, she'd kind of been hoping she'd be dragged in a totally different direction.

"We're going for a ride. We need to talk." She hadn't even noticed him grabbing her unused helmet from the top of the dresser, but there it was in his hands. He pushed it on her head, and donned his own. Before she knew what was happening, she was sitting behind him on the bike, his hands locking her own around his waist. Then they were moving before she had a chance to panic and jump off.

"Justin…I don't know about this," she squeaked, but

realized he didn't have a chance to hear her voice from inside the helmet, with the noise of the engine surrounding them. She held on tight, since there was no other choice, and rested her helmeted head against his back.

This wasn't so terrible, after all. His back was warm and steady against her, and despite the speed, she felt quite safe. In fact, she felt almost one with him as their movements mirrored that of the bike.

She was in love, wasn't she? Yes, dammit, she was.

"I love you, Justin," she murmured, tightening her arms around his waist, secure knowing he couldn't hear her. To her shock he slowed down so quickly she had to peer past his shoulder to see if there was a problem.

"What did you say?"

Justin's voice echoed in her ear. The world stood still for a moment, even at forty mph. She took a deep breath and spoke again, her voice trembling. "Justin, please tell me these helmets don't come with built-in microphones."

The bike turned off the road, into a side lane leading toward the forest.

"Of course they do."

"Oh."

"Yeah."

"I didn't know that."

"I suppose you didn't."

She strained to read the emotions in Justin's voice. Embarrassment? Panic? Surprise?

"Or I wouldn't have said…what I just said."

The bike came to a stop, and Justin jumped off, removing both their helmets and grabbing her hand. He grinned at her and pulled her hand, heading into the forest.

"Where are we going?"

"You'll see. Come on."

He wasn't even going to mention what she'd said? He was just going to ignore it? Relief battled disappointment as she let him pull her into the shade. Did he think it didn't mean anything? And where was he taking her, anyway?

They walked under the canopy of the trees, the silence only broken by the crackling sound of their feet kicking at the rug of dry leaves. It was a path that wasn't quite a path, overgrown with shrubbery and roots. Justin led the way, only releasing her hand to hold branches out of the way so they wouldn't hit her face. Sunlight filtered through the leaves high above, creating an eerie illumination.

Then finally, they ended up in a place not so dense with trees, where sunlight peered between the branches and warmed the ground. The autumn colors twinkled from the leaves, but the warmth was almost that of summer.

Justin sat down in the grass, dragging her with him. She was just getting comfortable when she found herself flat on her back.

"Justin…?" she asked, as he braced himself above her, his head blocking out the sunshine, and the dark eyes warm and tender.

"Will you tell me again?" he asked. "This time knowing I'll hear it?"

She closed her eyes. "No."

His lips were warm on hers, his hands even warmer. "Please," he whispered into her ear, and she had to smile, the hope that everything would be okay suddenly blossoming into certainty. She curled her fingers in his hair and yanked gently.

"I already did," she said. "You, however, did not. These things have to come in pairs. You know. Yin and yang."

Justin stopped kissing her, and she focused her eyes to find him staring at her with a mock terror. "You're right! I wouldn't want to disturb the balance of the cosmos."

"Exactly."

His fingers began to fiddle with the buttons on her shirt. She idly contemplated protesting.

Nah.

Justin grinned at her as he unfastened the last button. "What do you think? Do I say it now, or after I do unspeakable things to you?"

"How unspeakable?" she asked, her voice unsteady as she suddenly found herself without a shirt, and his fingers busy at the top button of her jeans. "What are you doing? Justin, you're not a secret exhibitionist, are you? This place better be as private as it looks."

Justin was still, not seeming in any hurry now that he had managed to get her shirt and jeans off. She shaded her eyes with her hand and peered at him. "Justin? Wasn't there a little something you were going to tell me?"

"That's quite a message."

He was reading her underwear. Thanks to a small accident and some gymnastics involving a slippery baby lotion bottle, her newly washed underwear had gone straight from the drawer back to the laundry basket. Which meant that today, of all days, she had to be wearing French reading material.

Laura closed her eyes and yanked a corner of her discarded blouse over her middle. She should throw those things away, and buy something…less readable. "You speak French?"

"Can't say I do. I read a bit of French. Never been able to get hang of the actual pronunciation."

"Okay. What does it say?" She squeezed her eyes shut and sent up a quick prayer that it wasn't anything too dirty.

"It says…uh…let me just take another look." He pulled at the blouse that modestly hid the reading material. "Hey, let go, I need to see."

"You already took a look. Just tell me what it says."

"I didn't quite get a good enough look. Translation is a complicated matter, you know. You need to study the text thoroughly, explore every nuance of the original meaning. There's a whole science to it."

Grinning, she let him pull the garment away and peer at the cheerful cursive. He traced the letters with a finger, frowning in concentration. "Let's see…"

She waited a whole twenty seconds before commenting on his exploration. She tapped the back of his hand with two fingers. "Justin, this isn't Braille."

"Oh. You're right. Sorry."

Not that he removed his hand. Not that she minded.

"Well? What does it say?"

"Ah… It seems to be a Biblical quotation."

A Biblical quotation? How bad could that be? She opened her eyes. "You mean something like 'Thou shall not covet thy neighbor's ass'?"

"Something like that." Humor flickered in his eyes. "Too late for that, anyway."

She punched him gently. "Justin, what does it say?"

"Well, it says something about abandoning hope."

Mortification was too mild a word for moments like these. "Oh, God."

Justin was shaking with silent laughter. "I don't suppose your parents bought you those?"

"No way." She swatted his shoulder. "And that's not the Bible, you pagan, it's Dante."

"Oh."

"Besides, if my parents had to pick a quotation for my underwear, it would be 'multiply and be fruitful.' They want more grandchildren. Badly."

"Hmm. They'll have Jenna soon."

Laura almost felt like screaming. "Will they? Aren't you jumping over a few formalities here?"

"You already agreed to marry me. I'm holding you to it. Don't you think they'll accept Jenna as their granddaughter?"

"Of course they will. They would," she corrected herself. "If you were to propose and if I were to accept, I mean. They'll be ecstatic. I mean, they would. They've been waiting for a little girl forever."

"And I suppose we could make Jenna an aunt someday."

"An aunt?"

"I know. Sounds weird."

"Imagine the burden of responsibility, to become an aunt as a toddler! I mean, an uncle is okay. An uncle plays football and tosses you up in the air. An aunt is a lot more respectable and prim. An aunt knits booties and gives you thermal underwear for Christmas."

"Do you suppose they teach knitting in kindergarten? She'll have to be a fast learner."

"Why, Justin, are you trying to tell me something? You're pregnant already?"

"No. Just in love."

"Finally!" Laura shouted to the treetops. She pushed at Justin until he was on his back, and climbed on top of him. She pinned his arms down. "Close, but no cigar. Say it, or I'll tickle you in that secret spot of yours."

His eyes widened. "You wouldn't use that against me. A secret I shared with you during a sensitive moment. You wouldn't…"

"I would."

Her hand began the slow journey down from his head to his middle, and Justin twisted free and grabbed both her hands. "I love you."

"You're just saying that because I was about to tickle you."

"Yes. But I do, anyway. I love you."

This time it sounded like he meant it. She smiled down at him. "I know. Now."

His dark gaze turned solemn as he looked up at her, squinting against the sun. "I couldn't tell you, before. I thought you were just thinking about Jenna when you agreed to marry me."

"Well, I thought *you* were just thinking about Jenna," she said softly. "You left me out of everything. You were even planning to move away."

"I'm sorry. I thought I was protecting you. But I guess I was really protecting myself. I didn't even want to admit how much it hurt that I might be losing you." He put his hand behind her head and pulled her down for a slow, sweet kiss. "But everything's okay now, isn't it?" he whispered. "Everything?"

"Yes. Everything's perfect."

He grinned, and pushed the hair out of her eyes. "Good. How do you like my motorbike?"

"It was kind of fun," she confessed. "I'd be willing to give it a second try. At least on the way home."

"Great. Want to know what else is fun?" His hand was on an away mission again.

"Tell me."

"French Braille."

"Don't you think we should finish our discussion first?"

Justin sighed and pulled his hands away. He stared at the sky, shading his eyes with his arm. "Okay. It'll kill me, but okay."

She played with the buttons on his shirt, idly unbuttoning them one by one. There had to be yin and yang in the undressing department, too. "Wonder what my mother will say?"

"Not much. Nothing's changed from her standpoint, and the wedding is still on for tomorrow."

Her hand stilled. "It is?"

He put his hand on her cheek and kissed her. "Isn't it? Will you marry me? Tomorrow?"

Her third proposal in one week, and finally one that didn't make her want to howl in despair. She leaned down and kissed him softly. "Yes."

Justin didn't seem completely satisfied by her answer, straightforward though it was. "You know it's not simple, Laura. There will be three of us. Are you sure you're ready to be a mother?"

"No, I'm not," Laura confessed. "No more than you're ready to be a father. But we'll do great anyway."

"We'll be a family."

Warmth spread through her. "Yes. A family."

"I've never tried that before."

She stroked a finger over the worried crease between his eyes. "Don't worry. It'll be fine. In fact, I suspect you're a natural."

"I love that kid so much," he said. "I'd never loved anyone since Ben. And now I love you *and* Jenna. Do you suppose my poor untried heart can handle all this work?"

She smiled and kissed his chest. "I promise—every time it hurts, I'll kiss it better."

An offer you can't afford to refuse!

High-valued coupons for upcoming books

A sneak peek at Harlequin's newest line— Harlequin Flipside™

Send away for a hardcover by *New York Times* bestselling author Debbie Macomber

How can you get all this?

Buy four Harlequin or Silhouette books during October–December 2003, fill out the form below and send the form and four proofs of purchase (cash register receipts) to the address below.

I accept this amazing offer!
Send me a coupon booklet:

Name (PLEASE PRINT)

Address   Apt. #

City   State/Prov.   Zip/Postal Code
                                                           098 KIN DXHT

Please send this form, along with your cash register receipts
as proofs of purchase, to:

In the U.S.:
Harlequin Coupon Booklet Offer, P.O. Box 9071, Buffalo, NY 14269-9071

In Canada:
Harlequin Coupon Booklet Offer, P.O. Box 609, Fort Erie, Ontario L2A 5X3

Allow 4–6 weeks for delivery. Offer expires December 31, 2003.
Offer good only while quantities last.

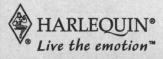

Visit us at www.eHarlequin.com

Q42003

Your opinion is important to us! Please take a few moments to share your thoughts with us about your experiences with Harlequin and Silhouette books. Your comments will be very useful in ensuring that we deliver books you love to read. *Please take a few minutes to complete the questionnaire, then send it to us at the address below.*

Send your completed questionnaires to:
Harlequin/Silhouette Reader Survey, P.O. Box 9046, Buffalo, NY 14269-9046

1. As you may know, there are many different lines under the Harlequin and Silhouette brands. Each of the lines is listed below. Please check the box that most represents your reading habit for each line.

Line	Currently read this line	Do not read this line	Not sure if I read this line
Harlequin American Romance	❑	❑	❑
Harlequin Duets	❑	❑	❑
Harlequin Romance	❑	❑	❑
Harlequin Historicals	❑	❑	❑
Harlequin Superromance	❑	❑	❑
Harlequin Intrigue	❑	❑	❑
Harlequin Presents	❑	❑	❑
Harlequin Temptation	❑	❑	❑
Harlequin Blaze	❑	❑	❑
Silhouette Special Edition	❑	❑	❑
Silhouette Romance	❑	❑	❑
Silhouette Intimate Moments	❑	❑	❑
Silhouette Desire	❑	❑	❑

2. Which of the following best describes why you bought *this book?* One answer only, please.

the picture on the cover ❑	the title ❑
the author ❑	the line is one I read often ❑
part of a miniseries ❑	saw an ad in another book ❑
saw an ad in a magazine/newsletter ❑	a friend told me about it ❑
I borrowed/was given this book ❑	other: _____ ❑

3. Where did you buy *this book?* One answer only, please.

at Barnes & Noble ❑	at a grocery store ❑
at Waldenbooks ❑	at a drugstore ❑
at Borders ❑	on eHarlequin.com Web site ❑
at another bookstore ❑	from another Web site ❑
at Wal-Mart ❑	Harlequin/Silhouette Reader
at Target ❑	Service/through the mail ❑
at Kmart ❑	used books from anywhere ❑
at another department store ❑	I borrowed/was given this ❑
or mass merchandiser	book

4. On average, how many Harlequin and Silhouette books do you buy at one time?

I buy _____ books at one time ❑
I rarely buy a book ❑

MRQ403HR-1A

5. How many times per month do you shop for any *Harlequin and/or Silhouette* books?
One answer only, please.

1 or more times a week	❑	a few times per year	❑
1 to 3 times per month	❑	less often than once a year	❑
1 to 2 times every 3 months	❑	never	❑

6. When you think of your ideal heroine, which *one* statement describes her the best?
One answer only, please.

She's a woman who is strong-willed	❑	She's a desirable woman	❑
She's a woman who is needed by others	❑	She's a powerful woman	❑
She's a woman who is taken care of	❑	She's a passionate woman	❑
She's an adventurous woman	❑	She's a sensitive woman	❑

7. The following statements describe types or genres of books that you may be
interested in reading. Pick *up to 2 types* of books that you are most interested in.

I like to read about truly romantic relationships	❑
I like to read stories that are sexy romances	❑
I like to read romantic comedies	❑
I like to read a romantic mystery/suspense	❑
I like to read about romantic adventures	❑
I like to read romance stories that involve family	❑
I like to read about a romance in times or places that I have never seen	❑
Other: _____	❑

*The following questions help us to group your answers with those readers who are
similar to you. Your answers will remain confidential.*

8. Please record your year of birth below.

19 ____

9. What is your marital status?

single ❑   married ❑   common-law ❑   widowed ❑
divorced/separated ❑

10. Do you have children 18 years of age or younger currently living at home?

yes ❑   no ❑

11. Which of the following best describes your employment status?

employed full-time or part-time ❑   homemaker ❑   student ❑
retired ❑   unemployed ❑

12. Do you have access to the Internet from either home or work?

yes ❑   no ❑

13. Have you ever visited eHarlequin.com?

yes ❑   no ❑

14. What state do you live in?

_____

15. Are you a member of Harlequin/Silhouette Reader Service?

yes ❑   Account # _____   no ❑   MRQ403HR-1B

It's romantic comedy with a kick
(in a pair of strappy pink heels)!

Introducing

"It's chick-lit with the romance and happily-ever-after ending that Harlequin is known for."
—*USA TODAY* bestselling author Millie Criswell, author of *Staying Single*, October 2003

"Even though our heroine may take a few false steps while finding her way, she does it with wit and humor."
—Dorien Kelly, author of *Do-Over*, November 2003

Launching October 2003.
Make sure you pick one up!

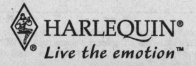

Visit us at www.harlequinflipside.com

LEGACIES . LIES . LOVE .

*The glamour and mystery of this
fascinating NEW 12-book series
continues in November 2003...*

RING OF DECEPTION

by favorite Harlequin Presents® author

Sandra Marton

Detective Luke Sloan was hard-edged, intimidating...
and completely out of his element working
undercover in the Forrester Square Day Care!
He was suspicious of single mom Abby Douglas...
but when he realized that her fear was over something—
or *someone*—far more dangerous than himself,
the man in him needed to protect her.

*Forrester Square...
Legacies. Lies. Love.*

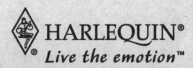

Live the emotion™

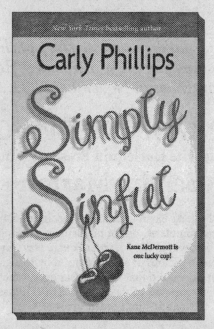
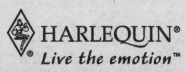